This is a work of fiction. Similarities to real people, places, or events are entirely coincidental.

THE SECRET SANTA'S LAST GIFT

First edition. December 14, 2024.

Copyright © 2024 Yash d..

ISBN: 979-8230515258

Written by Yash d..

Table of Contents

To those who believe in the magic of giving, To the quiet heroes who spread kindness without expecting recognition, And to the warmth of the community that shines brightest during the coldest days.

This story is for everyone who cherishes the spirit of Christmas, not in the gifts we receive, but in the love we share.

May this book remind you of the joy of togetherness and the beauty of giving from the heart.

With holiday cheer,

Yash D.

Preface

The holiday season has always been a time for miracles, warmth, and togetherness. It's a season that reminds us of the power of giving and the connections that bind us to one another. But what happens when a cherished tradition suddenly takes on a life of its own, unraveling the hidden stories and secrets of a community? That's the heart of *The Secret Santa's Last Gift*—a tale that celebrates the spirit of Christmas while weaving a mystery that will keep you turning the pages.

I wrote this book to capture the magic and meaning of the holidays, with a dash of intrigue and a sprinkling of festive wonder. Growing up, the smallest acts of kindness during the Christmas season always seemed to carry the greatest weight. They reminded me that even in our smallest gestures, we leave behind a legacy of love. This story reflects that idea: how a seemingly simple tradition, like a Secret Santa, can shape a town and its people in profound and unexpected ways.

In *The Secret Santa's Last Gift*, you'll journey to Winter Hollow, a town full of charm and character, where one person's selfless actions bring light and joy to an entire community. But when their sudden absence leaves behind a final, mysterious gift, the town must come together not just to discover its recipient, but to confront the truths that the gift reveals. It's a story of resilience, redemption, and the beauty of connection—perfect for readers who love cozy mysteries with a heartwarming holiday twist.

This book is best enjoyed curled up by a roaring fire, with a cup of hot cocoa in hand, surrounded by the glow of Christmas lights. Each chapter is crafted to immerse you in the festive spirit while unraveling a story that's equal parts suspenseful and heartwarming. My hope is that by the time you reach the final page, you'll not only have experienced a thrilling mystery but also felt the warmth of a community coming together in the truest spirit of Christmas.

As you read, remember the words of the Secret Santa: *The greatest gift isn't what we find under the tree—it's the love we give, the secrets we share, and the bonds we cherish.*

Thank you for joining me on this festive journey. May *The Secret Santa's Last Gift* fill your heart with joy, wonder, and a touch of Christmas magic.

Warm wishes,

A Town Wrapped in Red and Green

Winter Hollow was a place that seemed like it had been plucked straight from the pages of a Christmas card. Nestled between rolling hills blanketed in snow, the town glowed in hues of red and green during the holiday season. Strings of twinkling lights adorned every lamppost, wreaths hung proudly on each door, and the scent of freshly baked gingerbread lingered in the crisp air. The townsfolk took their festive traditions seriously, none more so than the beloved Secret Santa event. For decades, this cherished ritual had brought joy, laughter, and surprises to the community. Every December, an anonymous figure would leave gifts for residents, always managing to select something deeply personal and meaningful for each recipient. No one knew the identity of the Secret Santa, and no one dared to ask—it was an unspoken rule, a part of the magic.

This year, however, there was an extra layer of anticipation. Rumors had swirled that the Secret Santa might make an extraordinary announcement, revealing their identity or leaving behind one final grand gesture. Excitement buzzed in the air as the first snow of the season blanketed the town square, where the annual tree-lighting ceremony was about to begin. Families gathered, bundled in scarves and mittens, children clutching cups of hot cocoa as they waited for the towering spruce to come alive with light. The mayor, a jolly man with a booming voice and a perpetual twinkle in his eye, stepped up to the podium to address the crowd. "This year," he declared, "will be the most magical one yet for Winter Hollow!"

But the festive cheer was soon to be overshadowed by unexpected news. Just as the choir began to sing a spirited rendition of "O Holy Night," whispers began to ripple through the crowd. Faces turned somber as phones buzzed with the announcement that had just been shared: the town's beloved Secret Santa had passed away. Evelyn Carter, the sweet and sprightly woman who ran the general store, was the first to confirm it. "It's true," she said softly, her voice trembling. "John Whitaker is gone." John Whitaker. The quiet man who lived on the edge of town in a modest cottage surrounded by pines. Everyone knew him, of course, but no one had ever suspected he was the Secret Santa. His passing hit the town hard—not just for the loss of a neighbor but for what it meant for the tradition that had united them for so long.

The tree-lighting ceremony continued, but the joy seemed dimmed. People exchanged knowing glances and murmurs of sorrow, their hearts heavy with the news. How had John managed to keep such a secret all these years? Why had he chosen now, of all times, to leave? And, perhaps most importantly, what would become of the tradition? As the night wore on, the air of mourning began to mix with curiosity. It wasn't long before word spread that something unusual had been found in John's home—a gift. Not just any gift, but one marked as the last from the Secret Santa. A simple box, wrapped in crimson paper with a gold bow, sat on the small table by his fireplace. Attached to it was a note in John's neat handwriting: "To be delivered on Christmas Eve. For someone who truly needs it."

Speculation ran wild. Who was the gift for? What could be inside? The mystery took on a life of its own, spreading through Winter Hollow like wildfire. People couldn't help but share their theories, each more elaborate than the last. Some believed the gift was meant for a child, perhaps one who needed a bit of holiday magic to brighten their life. Others thought it might contain a message or keepsake that would reveal John's reasons for dedicating his life to this tradition. A few more practical-minded residents suggested it might be nothing more than an empty box, a symbolic gesture to remind the town of the importance of giving. But no one could say for sure, and the mystery only deepened as the days ticked by.

Despite the sadness of John's passing, something remarkable began to happen in the days leading up to Christmas. The town, instead of succumbing to grief, seemed to rally together. Inspired by John's legacy, the residents of Winter Hollow decided to honor the Secret Santa tradition in their own way. Families who had never exchanged gifts before began leaving small surprises for one another. Neighbors baked extra batches of cookies to share, and handmade cards found their way into mailboxes. The town square, once a place of quiet reflection after the news of John's death, was now bustling with energy as people shared stories about the mysterious gifts they had received over the years.

Evelyn Carter recounted how one year, a beautifully bound journal had appeared on her doorstep just when she had been struggling to write her first novel. It had been the encouragement she needed, and now she had three published books to her name. "That journal changed my life," she said, her voice thick with emotion. "John must have known." Another resident, George Manning, shared how he had received a pair of gloves during a particularly harsh winter. "I didn't have much money that year," he admitted. "Those gloves kept me warm—and reminded me that someone cared." Each story added another layer to the town's collective memory, painting a picture of a man who had quietly touched countless lives with his thoughtfulness and generosity.

As Christmas Eve approached, the town buzzed with anticipation. The mysterious gift remained in its place at John's cottage, guarded by his loyal dog, a shaggy golden retriever named Max. The mayor announced that the entire community would gather in the town square to witness the opening of the gift, a fitting tribute to the man who had brought so much joy to their lives. Snow fell softly that night, blanketing Winter Hollow in a pristine white that shimmered under the glow of the holiday lights. Families arrived early, bundling together for warmth as they sipped hot cider and exchanged hopeful smiles.

Finally, the moment arrived. Evelyn, accompanied by Max, carried the gift to the center of the square. A hush fell over the crowd as she carefully untied the golden bow and lifted the lid. Inside was a simple wooden box, intricately carved with symbols of peace and unity. Evelyn opened the box to reveal its contents: a stack of handwritten letters, each addressed to a different resident of Winter Hollow. Tears filled her eyes as she read the first one aloud. It was a heartfelt message from John, expressing his gratitude for the kindness and love he had received from the community over the years. Each letter contained a similar sentiment, a personal note to remind the recipient of their worth and the joy they had brought to others.

The town stood in silence, moved beyond words. John's final gift wasn't about material things; it was a reminder of the power of connection, of the importance of giving not just during the holidays but throughout the year. As the letters were distributed, smiles broke out, and hugs were exchanged. The warmth of the moment seemed to melt away the chill of the winter night. John Whitaker's legacy had not ended with his passing—it had transformed into something even greater, a bond that would continue to bring the town together for generations to come. Winter Hollow's lights seemed to shine a little brighter that Christmas, a testament to the enduring spirit of its Secret Santa.

The Secret Santa's Last Gift

The first snowfall of the season blanketed Winter Hollow in a soft, white hush, yet the usual cheer that accompanied the season was conspicuously absent. The bells strung up along Main Street jingled faintly in the cold wind, their sound a poignant reminder of a tradition that felt suddenly hollow. The heart of Winter Hollow, its beloved Secret Santa, was gone. Word spread faster than the snow fell, carried on whispers, gasps, and tearful murmurs. No one could believe it.

Everyone knew him—well, not exactly him, but his legacy. For twenty years, Winter Hollow had been enchanted by the magic of the Secret Santa. Each year, mysterious gifts appeared on doorsteps, in mailboxes, or hung from the sprawling branches of the town's giant Christmas tree in the square. These weren't just ordinary gifts; they were deeply personal, tailored to bring joy, solace, or even redemption. A single mother struggling to make ends meet would find a box of groceries and a new coat for her child. An elderly widow might receive a handwritten card filled with words of comfort, accompanied by her favorite tea. It wasn't just about the gifts—it was about the care, the thoughtfulness, the love that seemed to emanate from a person no one could name.

And now, the man behind it all, Mr. Harold Whitaker, was gone. He had been discovered that morning by his housekeeper, slumped in his armchair by the fire, a half-wrapped package on the table beside him. A heart attack, they said, quick and silent. The news hit like a snowball to the chest. For years, the townspeople had speculated about who the Secret Santa might be, but no one had ever guessed Harold. Quiet, reserved Harold, who ran the town's small post office and always seemed to be just another face in the crowd.

The revelation of his identity was a twist no one expected. It was like finding out that the tree at the center of the square had grown its own lights. Harold? The man who rarely joined in carol singing and preferred to sit on the sidelines during the town's annual Christmas parade? But as the shock wore off, memories began to surface. Mrs. Green, who ran the flower shop, recalled how Harold had always taken extra care with the mail in December, working late into the night. "He'd hum Christmas tunes under his breath," she said, wiping her eyes. "I thought he was just in the holiday spirit."

At the café, where the townsfolk gathered to share their disbelief, Mr. Patel, the hardware store owner, confessed he'd once seen Harold in the square late at night, standing by the tree. "I thought he was just admiring the lights," he admitted, his voice heavy with regret. "I didn't think... I didn't know..."

The weight of not knowing gnawed at everyone. How many lives had Harold touched? How many of them owed a piece of their Christmas joy to this quiet man? The realization brought tears and smiles in equal measure. But then, another question arose, whispered at first and then growing louder. What would happen now?

The package found next to Harold's chair became the center of speculation. Sheriff Taylor, who had taken charge of Harold's belongings, mentioned it in passing, and the town's curiosity ignited like a spark in dry kindling. The package, wrapped in glossy red paper and tied with a silver bow, bore a tag: *For Someone Special.* No name, no address, just those three simple words.

It was clear to everyone that this was Harold's final gift. The last offering from the man who had given so much to Winter Hollow. But who was it for? And what was inside? The mystery consumed the town. At the general store, theories flew faster than snowflakes. Some believed it was meant for a child, perhaps little Sophie Blake, whose father had been out of work for months. Others were convinced it was for Mrs. Thompson, the retired schoolteacher who had recently lost her home to a fire. And then there were those who thought it might be for no one in particular, a symbolic gesture to the entire town.

The more people speculated, the more the gift seemed to take on a life of its own. It became a beacon of hope and a source of tension. Old grudges resurfaced as people whispered about who deserved it most. The Johnson brothers, who hadn't spoken in years, accused each other of coveting the gift. Carol, the town's gossip, hinted that Harold might have left it for someone he secretly loved, setting tongues wagging about potential romantic entanglements.

Despite the rising tensions, there was something unifying about the mystery. For the first time in years, the entire town gathered in the square night after night, braving the cold to share stories about Harold and wonder about his final act of kindness. The giant Christmas tree stood tall above them, its lights twinkling like stars, as if Harold himself were watching from beyond.

Amid the discussions, small acts of kindness began to ripple through the town. Inspired by Harold's legacy, people started leaving anonymous gifts for one another. A pair of gloves appeared on the doorstep of the baker's apprentice, who had been shivering through his morning deliveries. A note of encouragement was slipped into the mailbox of the widower who had been struggling with loneliness. It was as though Harold's spirit had seeped into the very air of Winter Hollow, nudging its residents to carry on his tradition.

But the unanswered question of the red-wrapped package loomed large. Sheriff Taylor, who had kept the gift locked away in his office, found himself inundated with requests to open it. "It's not my decision to make," he said firmly, though his resolve was tested daily by the pleading eyes of townsfolk.

It wasn't until the town meeting, hastily convened on the eve of Christmas Eve, that a decision was made. The meeting was held in the town hall, its walls adorned with garlands and wreaths. Nearly every resident of Winter Hollow was in attendance, their breath visible in the chilly air as they crowded together. After much debate, it was decided that the package would be opened in the square on Christmas Eve, in the presence of everyone. It felt fitting, a final communal act to honor the man who had brought them so much joy.

As the day approached, the atmosphere in Winter Hollow grew electric with anticipation. The mystery of the gift became more than just a question of what lay inside—it became a symbol of everything Harold had stood for: love, generosity, and the belief that even the smallest acts of kindness could make a world of difference.

And so, as the clock ticked closer to Christmas Eve, the town held its breath. Snow fell softly over the rooftops, muffling the sounds of the world. The church bells rang out, their melody carrying through the frosty air. Somewhere, in a quiet corner of Winter Hollow, the final chapter of Harold Whitaker's legacy awaited its unveiling, ready to remind the town of the true meaning of Christmas.

A Mysterious Package

The snow had begun to fall in delicate, whisper-soft flakes over Winter Hollow, blanketing the small town in a layer of festive charm. Yet, the usual cheer that accompanied the season seemed muted this year. The passing of Arthur "Santa" Grayson, the town's unofficial Secret Santa, had cast a long shadow over the community. For decades, Arthur had been the heart of the town's Christmas celebrations. His jolly demeanor, kind acts, and knack for choosing the perfect anonymous gifts made him a beloved figure. His absence left a void that no amount of twinkling lights or carols could fill.

Arthur's quaint workshop stood at the edge of Main Street, its shutters closed tightly, as if in mourning. The townsfolk had always wondered about the magic that went on inside those walls, but Arthur guarded his secrets closely. This year, however, something had changed. As preparations began to organize his belongings, the late Santa's nephew, Charlie, who had arrived from the city to handle the estate, discovered a single package resting on Arthur's well-worn workbench.

The package was wrapped in silver paper that shimmered under the workshop's dim light, tied with a red ribbon and a tag that bore no name—just the words: "For You." It was unusual for Arthur to leave a gift unmarked. He had been meticulous in his generosity, ensuring each recipient felt uniquely chosen. The mystery of the package sparked a quiet stir among the handful of townsfolk helping Charlie sort through Arthur's things that chilly afternoon.

At first, the discovery didn't seem significant. Perhaps it was an unfinished gift or something Arthur hadn't gotten around to delivering. But the more they studied the package, the more questions arose. Why would Arthur leave a gift so carefully prepared and yet give no indication of whom it was for? Why had he not mentioned it to anyone, not even his closest confidant, Father Bernard? The intrigue was undeniable.

Word of the mysterious package spread quickly through Winter Hollow. By the next morning, the town square buzzed with speculation. At the diner, where old friends and young families gathered for steaming mugs of cocoa and holiday chatter, the conversations revolved around the package. Mrs. Everson, the librarian, was convinced it contained a rare book, possibly a long-lost treasure Arthur had stumbled upon. Young Emma, who worked at the post office, imagined it might be a proposal—Arthur's final romantic gesture to someone he secretly admired. Sam, the town carpenter, scoffed at such notions, believing it was simply a forgotten trinket. But even he couldn't help but feel a twinge of curiosity.

Meanwhile, Charlie found himself in a peculiar position. As much as he wanted to honor his uncle's memory, he was a practical man, unused to the whimsical traditions of Winter Hollow. The idea of the town becoming consumed by a single package puzzled him. Yet, every time he considered opening it and ending the mystery, something stopped him. Perhaps it was the reverence with which the townsfolk spoke of Arthur, or the feeling that this package, whatever it was, deserved its moment.

The town council decided to hold off on opening the gift, at least for now. Instead, they proposed organizing an event—a gathering where everyone could come together to reflect on Arthur's legacy and, perhaps, collectively decide the package's fate. Charlie hesitated but ultimately agreed. He knew enough about small-town life to realize that ignoring such a consensus could lead to whispers and resentment. Besides, a part of him was starting to wonder if the package might hold some answer to a question he hadn't yet formed.

In the days leading up to the event, the workshop became a site of quiet pilgrimage. Townsfolk would stop by to peek through its frosted windows, hoping for a glimpse of the package that had taken on an almost mythical status. Children pressed their noses against the glass, spinning tales about what might be inside. Was it a magic snow globe? A letter from Santa himself? The adults, too, weren't immune to the mystery's pull. Even pragmatic Sam found himself glancing at the workshop as he passed, his mind wandering to possibilities he wouldn't admit aloud.

On the evening of the gathering, Winter Hollow was alight with the warm glow of lanterns and the sound of carolers. The square had been transformed into a winter wonderland, with garlands strung across lampposts and the scent of spiced cider wafting through the air. The package was placed at the center of it all, on a small table adorned with holly and candles. The sight of it, so unassuming yet imbued with such significance, drew murmurs from the crowd.

Father Bernard began the evening with a heartfelt tribute to Arthur. He spoke of the man's generosity, his humor, and the way he brought people together. "Arthur believed that the true magic of Christmas wasn't in the gifts we give or receive but in the connections we nurture," Bernard said, his voice steady but tinged with emotion. "Perhaps this package is his final way of reminding us of that."

Charlie stepped forward, feeling the weight of a hundred expectant gazes. He cleared his throat. "I didn't know my uncle the way many of you did," he began, his voice tentative. "To me, he was the quirky man who sent me hand-carved ornaments every year, no matter how old I got. But being here, seeing the impact he had on this community, I realize how special he was. Whatever this package holds, I think it's meant for all of us in some way."

As the evening wore on, the townsfolk shared stories about Arthur, each one painting a vivid picture of a man who had quietly, persistently made their lives brighter. There was the time he replaced the broken swing at the park without telling anyone, and the year he anonymously donated books to the school library when budgets were tight. Each story seemed to weave a thread, connecting the community in a tapestry of shared love and gratitude.

By the time the crowd began to disperse, the package remained unopened. It seemed fitting, somehow, that the mystery lingered. For now, the gift wasn't just an object wrapped in silver paper. It was a symbol—a reminder of Arthur's legacy and the spirit of giving that bound Winter Hollow together.

As Charlie locked the workshop that night, he found himself smiling. The package was still a mystery, but he no longer felt the pressing need to solve it. In its own way, it had already given the town a gift: a reason to come together, to reminisce, and to remember what mattered most. The snow continued to fall, soft and steady, blanketing Winter Hollow in peace.

Names on the Naughty List

The snow fell softly on Winter Hollow, blanketing the town in a serene hush that belied the simmering tension brewing beneath its cheerful facade. The air smelled of pine and cinnamon, and the festive decorations sparkled against the icy glaze of winter. It should have been a season of joy and togetherness, but the unexpected passing of the town's beloved Secret Santa had cast a shadow over the holiday cheer. His sudden departure had left behind more than grief—it had left a mystery. One final, intricately wrapped gift, bearing no name but radiating significance, sat in the window of the town hall. It was the talk of the town, and everyone wanted to know who it was meant for and why.

The initial shock of the Secret Santa's death had brought the townspeople together, as grief often does. They reminisced about his selflessness, his uncanny ability to find the perfect gifts, and the way he seemed to know everyone's needs without asking. But as the days passed, curiosity about the mysterious gift began to sow seeds of speculation, and with it came whispers, assumptions, and old grudges that the community had long tried to bury.

In the bustling warmth of the Silver Bells Café, a hub for gossip as much as for coffee and pastries, conversations grew heated. "I bet it's for Mayor Hensley," said Clara, the owner of the flower shop, her voice tinged with suspicion. "He's always been cozy with Secret Santa. Probably rigged the whole thing to make himself look good." Across the table, Ruby, the librarian, scoffed. "That's ridiculous. If anyone's undeserving, it's you-know-who over at the bakery. Secret Santa might have been kind, but even he couldn't have overlooked that scandal from three Christmases ago." The air crackled with unspoken tensions as other patrons exchanged nervous glances.

Down by the hardware store, Tom, the gruff but good-hearted store owner, shared his theory with a group of regulars. "I'll tell you who it's not for: me. Secret Santa and I didn't exactly see eye to eye after that donation mix-up last year. If it's for anyone, it's probably Marjorie. She's always been his favorite." The mention of Marjorie, the widow who ran the town's charity drives, drew murmurs of agreement and dissent. Some thought she deserved it for her tireless work; others questioned her motives and hinted at hidden agendas.

Marjorie herself, unaware of the swirling theories, found her own suspicions creeping in. She remembered an incident from years ago when the town council had debated canceling the Christmas parade. Secret Santa had been adamant about keeping it alive, but not everyone had supported him. Could one of those dissenters have been involved in this mysterious gift? She felt a pang of guilt for even considering such a thought, but the curiosity gnawed at her.

Meanwhile, at the bakery, Martin was kneading dough with a force that betrayed his agitation. He had overheard whispers suggesting that he didn't deserve to be part of the Secret Santa tradition because of his "past." It was a vague yet persistent reference to a time when his business had struggled, and he had relied on the town's goodwill to stay afloat. He'd repaid every kindness tenfold, or so he thought, but it seemed some memories lingered longer than others. The insinuation stung, and he couldn't help but wonder if those spreading the rumors were the same ones vying for the gift themselves.

At the town hall, where the mysterious package sat in a place of honor, the tension was palpable. Every passerby paused to gaze at it, some with curiosity, others with envy. The town clerk, Evelyn, had taken it upon herself to "guard" the gift, though it needed no guarding. Her stern demeanor made it clear she didn't trust anyone, and her frequent, pointed comments about honesty and integrity hinted at her own suspicions. "It's not just about the gift," she told anyone who would listen. "It's about what it represents. And some people in this town don't deserve that kind of recognition."

The unraveling threads of unity reached the children as well. On the playground, kids repeated fragments of overheard conversations, turning them into games and taunts. "Your dad's on the naughty list!" one child shouted, pointing at another. "No, your mom is!" came the indignant reply. What had once been a community bound by shared traditions now felt like a patchwork quilt being pulled apart at the seams.

In the midst of the growing unease, a few voices tried to restore harmony. Father Matthew, the town's pastor, gave a sermon about the true meaning of Christmas, urging forgiveness and unity. "The gift, whoever it's for, is a symbol of generosity and love," he said. "Let's honor Secret Santa's memory by being the community he believed in." His words resonated with some, but others dismissed them as idealistic platitudes. "Easy for him to say," muttered Linda, the post office clerk. "He's not the one being accused of not deserving it."

The tension reached a boiling point during the town's holiday committee meeting. What was supposed to be a discussion about the upcoming Christmas Eve festivities devolved into a thinly veiled debate over the gift. "If it's for someone who's truly made a difference, then I think we all know who that is," said Doris, the retired schoolteacher, with a pointed look at Marjorie. Marjorie's cheeks flushed, but before she could respond, Clara interjected. "Oh, come on, Doris. Everyone knows Secret Santa had a soft spot for you because you taught him in school. Maybe he felt sorry for you." The room erupted in murmurs, some shocked, others amused, as the undercurrent of jealousy broke the surface.

By the time the meeting ended, the spirit of camaraderie that had always defined Winter Hollow felt like a distant memory. People left in small groups, whispering their theories and grievances. The snow continued to fall, its gentle beauty a stark contrast to the storm brewing within the community.

As the week wore on, the gift remained unopened, its mystery intact. But its presence had already done something profound. It had revealed the cracks in the town's foundation, the resentments and insecurities hidden beneath layers of holiday cheer. Yet, amid the chaos, there were glimmers of hope. A few people began to reflect on their own behavior, wondering if they, too, had been quick to judge or too eager to speculate.

Clara, who had been among the most vocal, found herself thinking about the time Secret Santa had left a bouquet on her doorstep when her shop was struggling. She had never told anyone about it, but it had meant the world to her. Maybe, she thought, the gift wasn't about who deserved it the most but about reminding them all of the kindness they had shared.

As Christmas drew closer, the town realized that the gift's true significance might lie not in what it contained but in the conversations it had sparked and the lessons it had brought to light. Still, the mystery remained, and the question lingered: who would ultimately receive the Secret Santa's last gift? And would it bring them joy—or reveal something even deeper?

The Bakery's Best-Kept Secret

Winter Hollow was famous for many things: its snow-dusted streets that looked like a postcard come to life, its cheerful carolers who braved even the iciest nights, and above all, its bakery, *The Sugarplum Haven*. Run by the ever-smiling Mr. Albert and his wife, Martha, the bakery had been the heart of the town for nearly three decades. Each Christmas season, the scent of freshly baked gingerbread, frosted sugar cookies, and warm cinnamon rolls wafted down Main Street, drawing in townsfolk like moths to a flame. This year, however, a strange undercurrent of tension hummed beneath the usual festive cheer, and it all seemed to start the day Mr. Albert discovered the mysterious package left behind by the late Secret Santa.

Albert had always been a private man, despite his public role as the town's unofficial holiday cheerleader. He and Martha had moved to Winter Hollow thirty years ago, appearing one summer as if by magic. The townsfolk were drawn to their warmth and kindness, and it wasn't long before *The Sugarplum Haven* became a staple of the community. But Albert had never shared much about his past, and no one had thought to question it—until now.

It all began when the town gathered for a meeting to discuss the mystery of the Secret Santa's final gift. The package, neatly wrapped in shimmering gold paper and tied with a red velvet bow, had been found on the counter of the bakery just after the Secret Santa's passing. A note attached to the box simply read, *"For the one who needs it most. Merry Christmas."* The ambiguity of the message, paired with the fact that it had been left at *The Sugarplum Haven*, threw the entire town into a frenzy of speculation.

"Why was it left at the bakery?" asked Mrs. Henshaw, the owner of the antique shop. "Do you think it's for Albert or Martha? Or maybe they're just holding it for someone else?"

Albert had chuckled nervously at the suggestion, waving it off as a misunderstanding. But his usual jovial demeanor seemed dimmer, his laughter a little strained. Martha, too, had appeared uncharacteristically quiet during the meeting, her hands twisting nervously in her lap. Their unease did not go unnoticed by the observant townsfolk, who began to whisper among themselves.

The murmurs grew louder in the following days. Theories swirled like snowflakes in the winter wind, each more dramatic than the last. Some believed the gift was meant for Albert, as recognition for his years of generosity. Others whispered that Martha was hiding something—why else would she avoid eye contact during conversations about the package? A few cynics suggested that the gift might contain evidence of some long-buried scandal.

The turning point came one frosty evening when young Clara, the baker's apprentice, accidentally stumbled upon something curious while helping Albert clean the bakery's storage room. She had been organizing a shelf of dusty recipe books when a faded photograph fluttered to the floor. It was an old black-and-white image of a much younger Albert, standing outside a bakery that wasn't *The Sugarplum Haven*. His arm was around a woman who was not Martha, and the two of them were smiling as if they had the world at their feet.

Clara didn't know what to make of the photo but couldn't shake the feeling that it was important. She slipped it into her apron pocket, intending to ask Martha about it later. When she finally broached the subject, Martha's face turned as pale as the powdered sugar on her famous Christmas éclairs.

"Where did you find this?" Martha asked, her voice trembling.

Clara hesitated, unsure if she had overstepped. "In the storage room, ma'am. I didn't mean to pry. I just thought you might want it back."

Martha stared at the photograph for a long time before letting out a heavy sigh. "Clara, there are some things about Albert's past that even the townsfolk don't know. And it's not my story to tell... but perhaps it's time he finally shared it."

The next morning, Martha approached Albert as he kneaded a batch of dough. She held the photograph out to him without a word. The moment Albert saw it, his hands froze mid-motion, and the color drained from his face. He took the photograph with trembling fingers, his eyes misting over as he stared at the image.

"It's been so long," he murmured, almost to himself.

Martha placed a gentle hand on his arm. "Albert, they're already talking. They deserve to know the truth, and so do you. Maybe this... this package is a sign. Maybe it's time to let go."

Albert nodded slowly, though his expression was one of trepidation. That evening, he closed the bakery early and invited a small group of trusted friends to join him and Martha by the warmth of their kitchen hearth. Among those gathered were Clara, Mrs. Henshaw, and the town's mayor, Mr. Whitaker, all of whom had been part of the Secret Santa committee.

As they sipped on cups of hot cocoa, Albert cleared his throat, his voice heavy with emotion. "I suppose I owe you all an explanation," he began. "Before Martha and I moved here, I lived in a small town not unlike Winter Hollow. I ran a bakery there too, with my first wife, Eleanor."

The room fell silent, save for the crackling of the fire.

"We were young and ambitious, dreaming of building a life together. But one winter, Eleanor fell gravely ill. I poured everything I had into caring for her, even as the bakery struggled to stay afloat. When she passed away just before Christmas, I couldn't bear to stay in that town any longer. I sold the bakery and left, wandering aimlessly until I found my way here."

Albert paused, his eyes glistening with unshed tears. "Meeting Martha saved me. She gave me a second chance at life, at love. But I never told anyone about Eleanor because... I thought leaving the past behind was the only way to move forward."

Martha squeezed his hand in silent support.

"But this package," Albert continued, gesturing to the mysterious gift on the table, "it's made me realize that the past has a way of finding us, no matter how far we run. I don't know if this gift is connected to Eleanor, or if it's meant for me, or someone else entirely. But maybe it's time to face whatever it holds, together."

As the group exchanged solemn glances, the tension in the room began to lift. Albert's confession had not only unveiled a hidden chapter of his life but also reminded everyone of the power of vulnerability and forgiveness.

The gift remained unopened that night, but the bakery's secret had been revealed, and the weight of it seemed to melt away like snow under the morning sun. The townsfolk's whispers turned to admiration for Albert's courage, and *The Sugarplum Haven* felt warmer than ever, its ovens glowing with a renewed sense of purpose.

In the days leading up to Christmas, the town rallied around Albert and Martha, helping them prepare for the busiest season of the year. And though the package still sat untouched on the counter, its presence no longer felt ominous. Instead, it seemed to symbolize hope—a reminder that even the deepest secrets can lead to redemption and that the spirit of Christmas is ultimately about love, community, and second chances.

A Christmas Clue

The first snow of the season blanketed Winter Hollow in soft white, muffling the usual hum of life and amplifying the sharp crunch of boots on the frosted ground. The townsfolk, still reeling from the unexpected loss of their beloved Secret Santa, Mr. Theodore Winslow, tried their best to immerse themselves in the familiar traditions of the holiday season. His absence, however, left a noticeable void. For decades, Theodore had been the heart of their festive celebrations, orchestrating the Secret Santa tradition with unparalleled dedication and joy. It wasn't just his carefully chosen gifts or the mysterious way he managed to deliver them without ever being seen; it was the love he poured into every detail, a love that united the entire town.

The discovery of the mysterious gift happened one chilly morning when Margaret, Theodore's long-time housekeeper, was tidying up his study. Nestled amidst a clutter of wrapping paper, ribbons, and vintage ornaments, she found an elegantly wrapped box, far more elaborate than the typical Secret Santa gifts Theodore was known for. The red wrapping paper shimmered under the light, and a golden bow sat atop the package with precision that spoke of Theodore's meticulous nature. Attached to the box was a note written in his unmistakable hand. Margaret hesitated, her breath catching as she read the words aloud to herself: *"To the one who needs it most—your answers lie where the first star shines."*

Margaret felt her pulse quicken. What could Theodore have meant? The phrasing was cryptic, yet it felt deeply intentional, as though Theodore had left behind a puzzle for the town to solve. Without wasting time, she brought the box and the note to the town square, where the townspeople were gathered for their morning coffee at the Frosty Mug Café. The café, usually a hub of cheerful chatter, grew quiet as Margaret entered, her face pale and her hands trembling slightly as she held the box aloft.

"It's from Theodore," she announced, her voice shaky. "I think it's his last gift."

The air in the room seemed to shift. Conversations halted, and every face turned toward the shimmering package in her hands. Excitement and confusion mingled in their expressions as Margaret placed the box on the counter and unfolded the note for everyone to see. The cryptic message was met with murmurs of intrigue.

"What does it mean, 'where the first star shines?'" asked Sam, the town's baker, his flour-dusted hands clutching his apron. "Is it some kind of riddle?"

"It has to be a clue," said Evelyn, the librarian, her eyes already gleaming with the thrill of unraveling a mystery. "Theodore loved puzzles, and he always had a way of making everything feel like an adventure."

As the townspeople crowded around, theories began to emerge. Some believed the "first star" referred to the North Star, a symbol of guidance and hope. Others speculated it might be tied to the town's Christmas traditions—perhaps the star atop the grand tree in the town square or the twinkling lights that lined the church steeple. Regardless of the interpretation, one thing was clear: Theodore's final gift was not just a present; it was an experience he wanted the town to share.

The box remained unopened, as though respecting the sanctity of Theodore's intention. Instead, the focus shifted to deciphering the note's meaning. Evelyn proposed they start at the town archives, combing through records and photographs that might hold a clue. Sam suggested they investigate the town square, where the towering Christmas tree adorned with a radiant star at its peak stood as the centerpiece of their holiday celebrations. Still others thought the answer might lie at St. Nicholas Church, where the evening carol service often concluded with a reflection on the significance of the Bethlehem star.

The spirit of collective curiosity swept through Winter Hollow like a fresh gust of winter wind. For the first time since Theodore's passing, the townspeople felt united not in grief but in the shared purpose of honoring his legacy. Families bundled up in scarves and coats, venturing out to explore the various sites that might hold answers. Children giggled as they scoured the snowy streets, their excitement infectious.

Meanwhile, Margaret couldn't shake the feeling that the clue was deeply personal, meant not just for the town but for someone specific. She replayed Theodore's words in her mind: *"To the one who needs it most."* Who among them needed something so profoundly that Theodore would single them out? Her thoughts wandered to the people in the community who had faced hardships recently: Clara, who had lost her job at the mill; young Peter, who struggled to fit in at school; or perhaps Joseph, the reclusive handyman who rarely ventured out of his workshop.

That evening, as the town gathered in the square to share their findings, the sense of camaraderie was palpable. Although no one had yet cracked the code, the search itself had become a bonding experience. Stories were exchanged, laughter echoed through the crisp night air, and for a moment, it felt as though Theodore was still among them, weaving his magic into their lives.

It was Clara who noticed the engraving on the town's clock tower—something she had never paid attention to before. Beneath the golden star-shaped weather vane at its peak were the words: *"Guidance to all who seek it."* Could this be the "first star" Theodore referred to? The town rallied to investigate, climbing the narrow staircase inside the tower until they reached the top. There, tucked inside a small compartment, they found another note written in Theodore's hand: *"You're on the right path. Look where the lights of kindness shine brightest."*

The crowd erupted in a mix of cheers and groans. Theodore's clues were leading them on a merry chase, but no one seemed to mind. The next day, they fanned out once more, seeking places where kindness had left its mark. Some visited the soup kitchen Theodore had often supported, while others checked the donation center where he had anonymously left gifts every December. Every discovery felt like a piece of Theodore's legacy, a reminder of the selflessness and joy he had spread throughout Winter Hollow.

As the mystery deepened, so did the bonds among the townspeople. Neighbors who rarely spoke began working together, pooling ideas, and sharing stories about Theodore's quiet acts of generosity. Hidden talents emerged—like Clara's knack for deciphering codes and Joseph's surprising knowledge of local history. By the time they reached the final clue, the entire town had transformed. What had started as a search for a mysterious gift had become a journey of rediscovery—not just of Theodore's impact, but of the strength and spirit of their community.

When the gift was finally unveiled, its contents were both simple and profound: a small wooden box containing letters Theodore had written to each member of the community. Each letter contained a personal message of gratitude, encouragement, or advice tailored to the recipient. For Clara, it was a reminder of her resilience and the hope that better days were ahead. For Peter, it was a story of Theodore's own struggles as a child, a reassurance that he too would find his place in the world. For Joseph, it was an invitation to step out of his solitude and rejoin the community that cared for him.

At the bottom of the box was one final note addressed to the entire town: *"The greatest gift is the love we share. Keep spreading it, and Winter Hollow will always shine bright."*

The townspeople stood in quiet reflection, tears mingling with smiles as they realized the true essence of Theodore's legacy. The gift was never about the box or its contents. It was about the journey, the connections rekindled, and the reminder that the spirit of Christmas lives not in material things but in the bonds that hold a community together. As they gathered around the tree that night, singing carols under the twinkling stars, Winter Hollow felt warmer than ever, wrapped in the enduring love of its Secret Santa.

Silent Night, Hidden Truths

The church bell struck midnight, its deep resonance echoing across the snow-covered town of Winter Hollow. The town, blanketed in a thick layer of snow, seemed to hold its breath, the cold and the quiet of the night giving everything an eerie stillness. The festive lights from the town square twinkled faintly through the frosty windows, a sharp contrast to the somber mood hanging in the air. Tonight, the town was gathered at St. Nicholas Church for an event that no one could have predicted—a midnight gathering that was bound to reveal secrets long buried.

The snowstorm that had swept through the evening had kept most people indoors, but for those who were brave enough to face the cold, the gathering at the church was a place of solemnity, mystery, and hope. In the days leading up to this moment, rumors had swirled through Winter Hollow about the final gift left by the beloved Secret Santa, who had passed away unexpectedly. It was a gift that held within it an answer to a question no one had dared to ask, and no one seemed quite ready to face the truth. But tonight, as the clock struck twelve, everyone knew that the truth would come to light, whether they were ready or not.

Inside the church, the pews were filled with townsfolk, their faces dimly lit by the glow of candles placed along the aisle. The air smelled faintly of pine and cinnamon, the familiar scent of Christmas that was meant to bring comfort, but tonight, it only made the silence feel heavier. The usual joviality of the season was absent, replaced by a quiet anticipation that seemed to vibrate in the very air. At the front of the church, near the altar, stood a single, small wooden box. It had been placed there earlier, and it was now the focal point of every eye in the room. The box was wrapped in simple brown paper, with no ribbon or bow to give it the festive touch that most gifts carried. It looked plain, almost inconspicuous, but everyone knew that it was anything but ordinary.

Marie, the town's librarian, sat near the back, her fingers nervously clutching the edge of her shawl. She hadn't wanted to come to the church tonight, but something had compelled her to do so. Her mind kept returning to the days when the Secret Santa's gifts had brought joy to the town. She had always felt a sense of wonder when she received her little surprises each year, never knowing who had sent them, only that they were thoughtful and kind. But now, as the reality of the late Secret Santa's passing weighed heavily on her heart, she couldn't shake the feeling that there was something more to the story—something hidden, something dark.

Across the room, Arthur, the town's mayor, stood with his arms folded across his chest, his face tight with uncertainty. He had been the one to call this meeting, the one who had insisted that they gather here at midnight. He had insisted that the townsfolk come together, that they face whatever truths the Secret Santa's last gift might reveal. But deep down, Arthur wasn't sure he was ready to hear those truths. The town had always been a place of warmth and peace, and the idea that one of their own might have been hiding something so sinister made him feel uneasy. His mind raced back to the years before the Secret Santa's passing, to the people who had come into the town and left under strange circumstances, to the things that had happened in the shadows, things that no one dared to speak of.

As the clock ticked on, and the moment for the unveiling of the gift drew closer, the door at the back of the church creaked open. It was Caroline, the town's baker, entering with her daughter in tow. Caroline's face was drawn, her usual warmth absent, replaced by a certain hesitation. She had always been the heart of the town, always the one to organize the Christmas baking contest and serve hot cider at the annual tree lighting ceremony. But this year, everything felt different. Her eyes met Marie's for a brief moment, and there was a knowing exchange between them, a silent understanding that neither of them wanted to acknowledge, but both knew was real.

"Good evening," Caroline said softly as she took her seat beside Marie. The young girl beside her was unusually quiet, her eyes wide with curiosity, but there was an apprehension to her that made Caroline's heart ache. She wanted to protect her daughter from the truths that were about to unfold, but she knew she couldn't shield her from everything. There were things that needed to be said, things that needed to be faced.

At the front of the church, Father Thomas stood beside the wooden box, his hands clasped in front of him. His white robes glowed softly in the candlelight, but the solemnity of the occasion seemed to weigh heavily on him. He had known the Secret Santa well, having seen them through the years in the quiet moments of confession, prayer, and reflection. Father

Thomas had always believed that the Secret Santa was a symbol of hope, of the belief that kindness could be found in the most unexpected places. But now, as the church filled with tension and the silence grew thick, he realized that the last gift wasn't just a symbol of goodwill—it was a key, one that might unlock the dark corners of the town's history.

As the town gathered around, the atmosphere thickened with anticipation. There was a ripple of movement as people shifted in their seats, trying to make sense of the silence, to fill the emptiness with something. Anything. Arthur cleared his throat, his voice breaking the stillness.

"I called this gathering tonight," he began, his words slow and deliberate, "because I believe it's time for us to come together. The Secret Santa's last gift is something we can no longer ignore. It's time to uncover the truth, for all of us." His gaze swept across the room, meeting the eyes of everyone present. "We all know that there are secrets among us. And tonight, we have the chance to heal, to move forward, to find redemption."

The room fell silent again, and for a moment, no one moved. The weight of Arthur's words hung in the air. It was clear that the time had come to face something uncomfortable, something no one had wanted to speak of. The long-buried truths that had shaped Winter Hollow's past were about to resurface, and no one could predict how they would change everything.

Father Thomas nodded gravely and began to speak, his voice a calm but firm whisper. "Let us take a moment to reflect. Let us remember that the spirit of Christmas is about love, forgiveness, and community. Whatever is in this gift, whatever secrets it may reveal, we must approach it with open hearts and minds."

Slowly, with a deep breath, Father Thomas reached for the brown paper-wrapped box, his hands trembling slightly as he untied the string. As the paper fell away, the contents of the box were revealed—a simple, hand-carved wooden ornament in the shape of a star, with intricate patterns etched into its surface. It wasn't much, and yet it was everything. The ornament was a symbol, one that had been passed down through generations of Winter Hollow's residents. It had been crafted by someone who had loved the town deeply, someone who had known its history, its pain, and its joy.

Caroline gasped softly as her hand flew to her mouth, and Marie's heart sank. The ornament was no ordinary decoration. It was a family heirloom, one that had been lost years ago. The star had belonged to the town's founding family, the same family that had disappeared under mysterious circumstances decades ago. No one had ever spoken of what happened to them, but there were whispers, rumors, that the family had hidden something away before they left, something that had never been found.

"Father," Caroline said, her voice trembling, "where did this come from? This... this is my family's ornament. My grandfather made it, before he disappeared."

The room seemed to hold its breath as all eyes turned to Caroline. The star, the lost family heirloom, had been found in the most unexpected place. It was the final gift from the Secret Santa—a gift that held the key to unlocking a mystery that had haunted the town for generations.

And with that revelation, the truth began to unravel. The connections, the secrets, and the betrayals that had been hidden for so long now came into the light. The past, once shrouded in silence, now whispered its confessions, and the bonds of Winter Hollow's community were tested. But amid the revelations, something beautiful began to take shape—an understanding that, despite the secrets, they were all still a family, still bound by love, still together in the spirit of Christmas.

The town would never be the same, but perhaps that was the very gift they needed—freedom from the past, a chance to rebuild, and the beginning of a new chapter.

As the bell tolled once more, the town of Winter Hollow found peace in the quiet truth that had been uncovered. And with it, they found their redemption.

The Bellringer's Dilemma

The bell was always his favorite sound—an echo of both solemnity and celebration, ringing through the heart of Winter Hollow, a town that always seemed to glow brighter when the snow fell. For Thomas Hargrove, the town's bellringer, Christmas had always been a time to reflect, to appreciate the closeness of his small community, and to hold fast to the traditions that bound them all together. As the caretaker of St. Thomas Church's ancient bell tower, Thomas had long been trusted with the responsibility of ringing the bell during the Christmas Eve service, an honor passed down through generations of his family. But now, standing in the dimly lit tower and gazing out over the snow-covered rooftops, he couldn't shake the unease gnawing at him.

The town was quiet, save for the soft murmur of conversations down below as people prepared for the holiday. Yet, there was an underlying tension in the air, a quiet restlessness that had settled over Winter Hollow ever since the sudden death of their beloved Secret Santa. The man behind the town's cherished tradition had passed away unexpectedly, leaving only one final, mysterious gift behind. A gift wrapped in a humble brown paper with a single ribbon, its recipient unknown, its contents still a mystery.

Everyone in town had their theories. Some thought it was for the mayor's wife, a woman known for her constant charity work. Others suggested it might be for young Emily Saunders, the sweet baker's daughter who had been spreading Christmas cheer all year long. But there was one person who knew the truth—the one person who had always been close to the Secret Santa, the one person who could have known the identity of the intended recipient.

Thomas Hargrove.

The gift, left under the bell tower, was his responsibility. The late Secret Santa had asked him to keep it safe, to ensure it was given to the right person at the right time. But Thomas had been torn ever since. The gift wasn't just an ordinary present—it was a symbol, something more than just a simple token. It held a deeper meaning, something that could change everything for someone in the community. The town had always prided itself on the bonds they shared, but now, with the Secret Santa gone, those bonds seemed fragile, delicate, like they might shatter under the weight of secrets better left buried.

He had been told not to reveal who the gift was meant for, not yet. And he had kept his word. But now, with the town so close to uncovering the truth, Thomas found himself caught between loyalty and honesty. He had promised his late friend that he would keep this secret until the time was right, but with the town in turmoil, was it fair to keep the mystery alive?

His hands trembled slightly as he adjusted the ropes that controlled the bells. It had been a long day. The wind howled outside, sending gusts of snow through the narrow gaps in the old church windows. But inside the tower, Thomas was alone with his thoughts, with the weight of the town's curiosity pressing down on him like the cold winter air.

He had always been a man of few words, a quiet observer in the background of Winter Hollow's vibrant community. But now, he was at the center of a mystery he hadn't asked for, one that seemed to pull everyone closer together even as it threatened to tear them apart. People had started visiting the church more frequently, offering theories about the gift, about its meaning. They had come to him, their eyes full of hope and curiosity, expecting him to know something, to offer a clue that would unlock the mystery.

Thomas had always answered with a soft smile and a shrug, but inside, he was growing more anxious. What would happen if the gift was revealed too soon? What if it was never meant to be opened? What if the mystery was part of the magic, part of the Christmas spirit that made Winter Hollow so special?

He thought about the conversations he'd overheard down at the local diner, where everyone seemed to have their own theory about who the gift was for. The town's gossip, usually lighthearted and harmless, now seemed to be taking a darker turn. People were becoming impatient. The festive spirit that had once filled the air now seemed to be tainted by suspicion and anxiety.

And then there was Lydia.

Lydia had been a close friend of Thomas's for many years. She had always been the one person he could confide in, the one who understood the weight of the traditions he carried. She had known the Secret Santa too, back when he was alive, and she knew how important it was to keep certain things private. But Lydia was also the one person who urged him to break his silence, to reveal the truth before it was too late.

"You can't keep this secret forever, Thomas," Lydia had said just a few days ago, her voice filled with concern as they sat in the small parlor of her home. "The town deserves to know. You can't just keep hiding behind this mystery. It's not healthy for anyone."

But Thomas wasn't sure. The Secret Santa had left instructions for a reason. Perhaps it wasn't his place to reveal the gift's contents—perhaps it wasn't even meant for the whole town to know. But now, as Christmas Eve approached, Thomas felt a pressure that grew heavier with each passing hour. The gift was something more than just a present—it was a reminder of the bonds they all shared, a symbol of the kindness and generosity that made Winter Hollow unique.

As the clock struck six, signaling the start of the evening service, Thomas climbed the stairs to the bell tower. The light from the candlelit church below flickered softly through the windows, casting shadows on the snow-covered streets. He stood there for a moment, the ropes in his hands, his thoughts clouded by doubt.

The bells tolled, their sound echoing across the town. But as the sound rang through the streets, something in Thomas's heart felt hollow. He knew what he had to do. The decision had been made for him. The town could no longer be kept in the dark. It was time to reveal the truth.

Later that evening, as the town gathered for the Christmas Eve service, Thomas stood at the back of the church, watching the townspeople as they whispered excitedly among themselves. The mystery of the gift was the talk of the evening, and though no one yet knew the truth, there was a palpable sense of anticipation in the air.

Thomas felt Lydia's presence beside him, her hand resting lightly on his arm. She had always been there for him, but tonight, she seemed more distant, as if she, too, was waiting for the inevitable revelation.

"Are you sure about this?" she asked softly.

Thomas nodded, his gaze fixed on the crowd. "It's the right thing to do. They deserve to know."

With a deep breath, he turned and made his way to the front of the church. The room fell silent as he approached, the town's eyes all turning to him. He held up the mysterious gift, the brown paper gleaming under the soft glow of the candlelight.

"This," he said, his voice steady despite the uncertainty in his heart, "was the last gift our Secret Santa left behind. And tonight, I believe it's time for all of us to learn who it was meant for."

The air was thick with suspense as Thomas slowly unwrapped the gift, revealing a small, delicate wooden box inside. As he lifted the lid, the crowd gasped in unison.

Inside the box was a simple silver key, no bigger than a finger. And with it, a note that read:

"For the one who has always been the heart of Winter Hollow. The key to a future brighter than you can imagine. Merry Christmas."

The room fell silent. No one spoke. The mystery wasn't over, but for the first time in weeks, the tension in the air seemed to dissolve. The townspeople exchanged glances, their expressions a mix of confusion, wonder, and a dawning sense of realization.

The key, Thomas knew, wasn't just for anyone—it was for the person who had given the most to the town without ever asking for anything in return. It was the key to a future of hope, a future built on trust and community. And as the town looked around at one another, they began to understand that the gift was not just a symbol of giving—it was a reminder of the love that had always existed in Winter Hollow, a love that could never be undone.

And as Thomas looked out over the crowd, he knew that the real gift was not the key or the mystery—it was the sense of belonging that they had all found in each other, the gift that could never be taken away.

The bell rang once more, but this time, it was a sound of celebration, a sound of hope, and a sound that would echo through Winter Hollow for years to come.

Under the Mistletoe

The wind howled as snowflakes danced in the air, swirling around the town of Winter Hollow. It was Christmas Eve, and the town had never looked more magical. The streets were aglow with festive lights, and shop windows displayed carefully crafted decorations. The scent of freshly baked gingerbread and pine trees filled the air, and every corner of the town was wrapped in the warmth of holiday cheer. But beneath the sparkling exterior, there was a tension that had begun to spread throughout the community.

The unexpected passing of Winter Hollow's beloved Secret Santa had left everyone stunned, and now, with his last gift still a mystery, the town was in a frenzy. Everyone had their theories, their suspicions, and their hopes. It wasn't just about the gift itself; it was about the man who had been the heart and soul of this Christmas tradition. He had given without asking for anything in return, never revealing his identity, always making sure that the holiday spirit lived on in Winter Hollow.

But now, with the mystery of his final gift hanging in the air, something else was brewing beneath the surface. Something far more complicated, far more personal. The search for the recipient of the last gift had brought out emotions in people that they hadn't expected, and as they got closer to uncovering the truth, long-buried feelings began to surface.

Clara Westbrook stood in front of her small café, the snow falling lightly on her red scarf, her breath visible in the cold air. The café was beautifully decorated with strings of fairy lights, and a large mistletoe hung above the doorway, a perfect symbol of the festive season. She'd always loved Christmas, and this year, especially, she felt the spirit of it all. But that didn't make the situation any easier. The recent events had stirred up more than just excitement over the mystery gift; they had stirred up old emotions.

Clara had known for a long time that Winter Hollow was a place where secrets weren't always kept. People in small towns had a way of knowing things about each other, things they would rather not know, but it was the relationships that truly defined the town. Clara herself had lived here her entire life, running the café her father had started. She was used to the rhythm of the town, the familiar faces, the simple comforts of knowing everyone's story. But lately, her own story had become tangled with someone else's.

It had all started with the search for the Secret Santa's final gift. It was the one thing everyone could focus on, the one mystery that kept everyone on their toes. But for Clara, it had also meant seeing Ethan Fitzgerald again. Ethan had been her childhood friend, someone she had once been so close to that it seemed impossible to ever be apart. But life, as it often does, had other plans. Their paths diverged, and they hadn't spoken in years. That is, until the night of the Secret Santa's passing.

Ethan had been back in town visiting his parents for the holidays when the news broke. The moment Clara had seen him standing in front of the café, looking as handsome as ever, she felt a flutter in her chest. The same flutter she had felt all those years ago when they had been inseparable. But things were different now. Time had changed them both. They had both grown, both moved on in different ways. And yet, there was something in the air between them, something unspoken but undeniable.

"Clara," Ethan had said that night, his voice deep and warm, just like she remembered. "I didn't expect to see you here."

Clara had smiled, though it was a little forced. "I didn't expect to see you, either."

And just like that, it was as if no time had passed at all. The conversation flowed easily, the old familiarity between them slipping back into place. But with every word they exchanged, Clara felt something shifting inside her. Ethan was no longer just the boy she had grown up with. He was a man now, with the kind of presence that made everyone stop and take notice. He had always been charming, but now there was a quiet strength in him, a calm confidence that made Clara's heart skip a beat.

The town's search for the Secret Santa's last gift had pulled Ethan and Clara into a team, working together to follow clues and try to piece together the mystery. But the more time they spent together, the more complicated things became. Old feelings resurfaced, and the lines between friendship and something more blurred in ways neither of them had expected.

As the night of Christmas Eve drew closer, Clara found herself spending more time with Ethan than anyone else. They met regularly to talk about the gift, exchanging ideas and theories. But in the quiet moments between the discussions, when their eyes met across the table or when their hands brushed as they reached for the same coffee cup, there was an electric tension that neither could ignore.

It was one evening, as they were walking together down the snow-covered street, that Clara felt a surge of emotion. She wasn't sure what to call it—was it regret, longing, or something even deeper? The snow crunched beneath their boots as they strolled under the glow of the streetlights, their breaths visible in the cold air.

"You've changed, Ethan," Clara said softly, breaking the silence between them. "I can't quite place it, but there's something different about you."

Ethan stopped walking, his breath fogging in the cold air. "Maybe it's just time, Clara. You know how life is. You move away, you grow up, and you realize some things are worth revisiting."

Clara looked at him, her heart racing. "And what about us? Is that something worth revisiting?"

Ethan smiled, a hint of sadness in his eyes. "I don't know. But I think we both have unfinished business, don't we?"

The words hung in the air between them, and Clara felt a rush of emotions flood over her. She had never stopped thinking about Ethan, never stopped wondering what could have been if they had made different choices. But now, with everything so uncertain, with the mystery gift looming over their heads, Clara wasn't sure if this was the right time to revisit the past.

But fate, as it often does, had a way of pushing them in the direction they needed to go.

As the clock struck midnight on Christmas Eve, the town gathered in the town square, all of them eagerly awaiting the reveal of the Secret Santa's final gift. The air was thick with anticipation, and the crowd buzzed with excitement. Clara stood near the town's Christmas tree, the mistletoe still hanging above her head, and found herself looking around for Ethan. He hadn't arrived yet, and she couldn't help but feel a sense of disappointment.

Just as she was about to check her phone, she felt a hand on her shoulder. She turned to find Ethan standing there, his eyes soft in the glow of the Christmas lights.

"You weren't going to start the festivities without me, were you?" Ethan grinned, his voice filled with warmth.

Clara smiled, feeling a flutter of relief. "I was starting to wonder where you were. I thought I might have to open the gift without you."

"Well, I'm here now," Ethan said, his voice low and teasing. "And I don't think that gift will be the only thing we'll be opening tonight."

Clara's heart skipped a beat. As the crowd gathered around the stage to watch the unveiling of the gift, she and Ethan stood beneath the mistletoe. For a moment, everything else seemed to fade away. It was as if time had stopped. And then, without thinking, Clara leaned in, her lips meeting his in a soft, tentative kiss.

For that brief moment, everything felt right. The world around them disappeared, and all that mattered was the connection between them, the promise of something new, something unexpected.

The crowd cheered as the gift was revealed, but Clara didn't care about that. She cared about what had just happened beneath the mistletoe. As she pulled back slightly, she looked into Ethan's eyes, searching for answers to questions she hadn't yet voiced.

"I guess some things are worth revisiting after all," Ethan said, his voice soft and full of meaning.

And in that moment, Clara realized that the mystery of the Secret Santa's last gift wasn't the only secret worth unraveling. Sometimes, the greatest gifts were the ones you least expected, the ones that came wrapped in emotions you hadn't planned for, under the mistletoe of Christmas Eve.

The snow continued to fall gently around them, and the town of Winter Hollow, with all its secrets, mysteries, and newfound love, continued to shine brighter than ever before.

The Holly and the Ivy

As the heavy snow fell in gentle drifts outside, Winter Hollow was wrapped in a blanket of quiet anticipation. The town had always been filled with holiday cheer, but this year, there was an undercurrent of mystery that stirred among the residents. For weeks, they had wondered about the last, mysterious gift left behind by their beloved Secret Santa, who had passed away unexpectedly. Everyone in town knew the legend—the tradition that had been passed down through generations, where one anonymous person would leave gifts for others, spreading love and goodwill during the Christmas season. But now, with the passing of their Secret Santa, the town had no idea who had received the final gift or what it contained.

The truth, however, was buried in more than just the snow. It was hidden in an old diary—one that had been left behind by none other than Caroline Porter, the widow who had lived in the town's grandest house many years ago. Caroline had been known for her generosity and deep connection to the town's Christmas traditions. But after her sudden death years ago, her house had remained empty, and the townsfolk had mostly forgotten her legacy. It wasn't until a local antique dealer, Henry Watson, stumbled upon the diary in an old chest in the attic that the first clues started to surface.

Henry had never known Caroline personally, but when he flipped through the faded pages of her diary, something caught his eye—an entry dated December 24th, many years ago. The words were simple, but they carried weight: "The Holly and the Ivy are two sides of the same coin. Tonight, the gift will be revealed." It was strange and cryptic, but it had something to do with the Secret Santa mystery. Henry, feeling a mixture of curiosity and caution, decided to dig deeper into Caroline's past.

Caroline's house was a mansion on the edge of Winter Hollow, nestled near the woods that bordered the town. The house, now abandoned, had once been the hub of activity during the Christmas season. Caroline, with her sharp mind and generous heart, had started the Secret Santa tradition many years ago. It was said that she would secretly leave gifts for the families in need, taking care to ensure that each person received something special. No one ever saw her doing it, and no one knew her identity. It became a beloved part of the town's holiday spirit.

But what of the connection between Caroline's diary and the present mystery? What did the words "The Holly and the Ivy" really mean, and how did they tie into the final gift?

That afternoon, Lucy Bellamy, one of the town's most dedicated local historians, decided to investigate the mystery further. She had always been fascinated by Winter Hollow's history, and the diaries of Caroline Porter were something she had heard about for years but never truly explored. She made her way to Henry's antique shop, where he had promised to show her the diary.

As she walked into the shop, a wave of nostalgia swept over her. The shelves were filled with all sorts of treasures—old books, trinkets, and furniture, some valuable, some just pieces of the past waiting to be rediscovered. Henry was sitting at the counter, polishing an old silver teapot, and smiled warmly as Lucy approached.

"I've been waiting for you," he said, gesturing to the back corner of the shop where a dusty box sat. "The diary's in there. It's not much to look at, but it has some intriguing passages."

Lucy sat down at the table, eagerly flipping through the pages. The diary's leather cover was cracked with age, and the pages inside were yellowed with time. She found the entry Henry had mentioned and read it aloud to herself: "The Holly and the Ivy are two sides of the same coin. Tonight, the gift will be revealed."

Lucy pondered the meaning of the entry. The holly and the ivy were two common plants associated with Christmas, often used in decorations during the holiday season. But what was the connection? Why had Caroline chosen to leave such a cryptic message in her diary?

She continued reading, hoping for more clues. As she flipped through the pages, she came across another entry that seemed to hold more significance. This one was dated the year before Caroline's death.

"It's time," the entry began. "I've chosen the last recipient for my gift. But not all gifts are meant to be seen. Some are meant to heal. Some are meant to bring redemption. The holly and the ivy will guide them to the truth."

Lucy's heart raced. "Redemption?" she muttered to herself. "Could it be?" She knew that Winter Hollow had its fair share of secrets—old grudges and unresolved issues that had never been fully addressed. But what did Caroline's gift have to do with them?

The more Lucy thought about it, the more the pieces of the puzzle seemed to fit. She had heard whispers over the years of people who had received unexpected kindness from the Secret Santa, people who had been struggling or lost. Was it possible that Caroline had used her final gift to right a wrong, to mend a broken relationship, or even to help someone who had fallen into despair?

Lucy looked up at Henry, who was watching her carefully. "What do you think Caroline meant by this?" she asked, pointing to the diary entry.

Henry scratched his chin thoughtfully. "I don't know for sure," he admitted. "But I've always thought Caroline had a way of seeing the deeper meaning in things. She didn't just give gifts to make people happy. She gave them to help people find peace."

Lucy felt a chill run down her spine as she read one last entry. It was short, but the words were chilling. "The gift will be revealed when the town comes together. The holly and the ivy will point the way."

Suddenly, everything clicked. The holly and the ivy were not just decorations—they were symbols, representing two aspects of the same idea. Caroline had understood the importance of unity in the community. The town had been divided by old wounds for years, but Caroline had always believed that the town could heal if everyone worked together. The final gift, then, was a symbol of that healing.

But who was the recipient? And what was in the gift?

Lucy knew she had to act fast. The town was buzzing with speculation, but only a few people knew the full story. She couldn't wait any longer. She closed the diary and stood up.

"I think I know where the gift is hidden," she said, her voice steady with certainty. "And I know who it's for."

As she left the antique shop, Lucy's heart raced. The secret was finally within reach. She made her way to the old town hall, a place she hadn't visited in years. The holly and the ivy were there, hanging on the walls, symbols of the town's shared past and a future full of promise. As she entered the building, she felt a sense of calm wash over her. She wasn't just unraveling the mystery of the gift; she was uncovering a piece of the town's soul.

Inside the hall, a single wrapped package sat on a table, waiting to be discovered. Lucy approached it with caution, knowing that this was the moment of truth. As she carefully untied the ribbon, she was filled with a sense of wonder. The contents of the gift were simple, yet profound—a small wooden carving of a holly wreath and an ivy vine intertwined.

In that moment, Lucy understood. This wasn't just a gift. It was a message. A reminder of the power of community, of healing, and of the enduring spirit of Christmas. The holly and the ivy were symbols of unity—two parts of a whole that could never be separated.

The last gift of the Secret Santa wasn't about material value. It was about something far more precious: the redemption of a town that had forgotten how to come together. And now, as the snow continued to fall outside, Lucy knew that the town of Winter Hollow would never be the same again.

A Snowstorm of Secrets

As the snowflakes swirled outside, the town of Winter Hollow was suddenly thrown into disarray. What had started as a light dusting soon turned into a full-blown snowstorm, catching everyone off guard. The wind howled through the streets, whipping the snow into swirling gusts, obscuring visibility and making travel impossible. The local inn, always a gathering place for the townspeople during the holidays, was quickly becoming a sanctuary for those who couldn't make it home.

Inside, the warmth of the hearth did little to mask the tension that had settled over the group gathered around the fire. The storm had trapped them together, and it was clear that the long-overdue conversations and confrontations were finally about to take place. A group of old friends and acquaintances who had lived in Winter Hollow for years, each with their own secrets and regrets, now had no choice but to face them. The death of the beloved Secret Santa had already shaken them to their core, but the discovery of the final mysterious gift left behind by him had sent ripples of uncertainty and guilt through the entire town.

Maggie, the local bakery owner, sat close to the fire, her hands wrapped tightly around a steaming mug of hot cocoa. She kept her eyes on the flames, her mind racing. Just yesterday, she'd received a letter from the late Secret Santa, a letter she had never told anyone about. The letter had been tucked inside the final gift he'd left behind. As far as Maggie knew, the gift was meant for someone else in the community. But the contents of that letter made her wonder if she was the one who was truly meant to receive it. Maggie had always been the heart of Winter Hollow, baking sweet treats for everyone, and offering a warm smile no matter the weather. But now, with the snowstorm keeping everyone in one place, Maggie knew it was time to finally confront the secrets she had hidden away for so long.

Across the room, George, the local librarian, shifted uncomfortably in his seat. The storm was keeping everyone inside, but it was also making it harder for him to ignore the fact that he had been avoiding the truth for years. George had been a close friend of the Secret Santa, and the gift left behind had stirred up old feelings of guilt and loss that he wasn't sure he was ready to face. His mind kept returning to the moment when he and the late Santa had fallen out, a rift that had never been healed. As the snow continued to fall, George knew this was his chance to make amends, but the fear of facing his mistakes kept him silent. He had never been good at confrontation, and the weight of the past was heavy on his shoulders.

In the corner of the room, Rachel, the town's florist, watched the others carefully. She was quiet, but her eyes were sharp. Rachel had always been observant, noticing things that others overlooked, and tonight was no different. She had known the Secret Santa longer than anyone, and she suspected that the gift wasn't just meant to bring joy—it was meant to settle old scores. As the storm raged outside, Rachel couldn't help but wonder if she was included in that reckoning. There were things she'd done, things she had never spoken of, and now, with nowhere to go and no way to escape, she feared that the snowstorm was a metaphor for the storm of truths that was about to unfold.

Finally, sitting closest to the door, was Clara, the quiet and reserved schoolteacher who had never been one to engage in the town's gossip or drama. But as the storm trapped everyone inside, Clara felt the weight of the moment bearing down on her. She had a secret too, one that tied her to the very heart of Winter Hollow's holiday traditions. For years, she had kept it hidden from her neighbors, her friends, and even from herself. But tonight, something was different. The energy in the room had shifted, and she could feel it in the air. The storm outside was no longer just a weather event—it was a symbol of the emotions building within the room. Clara had no idea how or when she would speak the truth, but she knew that tonight would change everything.

The fire crackled in the background, casting a soft glow over the room as the group sat in silence. The wind howled outside, and the snow battered against the windows, but inside, the tension was palpable. No one dared speak first. Maggie's fingers tightened around her mug, and George fidgeted in his chair. Rachel stared out the window, her mind racing, while Clara sat with her hands folded tightly in her lap, staring at the floor. It wasn't just the storm outside that kept them trapped—it was the storm within, a storm of secrets that had built up over the years and now, with no escape, were finally coming to light.

The silence stretched on until Maggie could take it no longer. She set her mug down with a soft clink and took a deep breath. The words were stuck in her throat, but she knew she had to speak. For the first time in years, Maggie allowed herself to feel vulnerable. She couldn't keep running from the truth, and the storm outside was the perfect metaphor for the storm of emotions she had been avoiding. Her voice was soft but steady as she spoke.

"I have something to tell you all," Maggie began, her gaze fixed on the fire. "I was the one who received the last letter from the Secret Santa. It wasn't meant for anyone else in the town." She paused, letting the weight of her words settle into the room. "But I don't know if I should have kept it. I don't know if I should have told you."

The room fell into an even deeper silence as the others processed what Maggie had just revealed. George's eyes widened in shock, his mouth opening and closing as though he were unsure of how to respond. Rachel's sharp gaze flickered over to Maggie, but she remained silent, watching carefully. Clara, too, seemed to have been struck by the revelation, her face paling as she slowly looked up from her lap.

Before anyone could speak, the door to the inn swung open with a gust of wind, and in walked a familiar figure. Mayor Thompson, the town's leader, was soaked to the bone from the snow, his face flushed from the cold. He closed the door behind him with a thud, and the group turned toward him.

"Is it true?" the mayor asked, his voice tinged with both curiosity and urgency. "Did the Secret Santa leave behind something more than just a gift?" His eyes scanned the room, landing on each of them in turn. "Because I've been wondering... Was the gift really for someone else, or is it meant for all of us?"

The question hung in the air, and for a long moment, no one answered. The storm outside seemed to roar louder, as if echoing the turmoil inside the inn. The room was charged with the energy of unspoken truths, and Maggie realized with a sinking heart that no one would leave until those truths were exposed.

The snowstorm was not just a physical barrier—it was a mirror to the emotional storm that had built up in Winter Hollow over the years. As the group sat together, each person knew that this night would mark a turning point for the town. The snow would eventually melt, and the storm would pass, but the secrets that had been hidden for so long would change Winter Hollow forever.

The Ornament's Message

I t was the second day after the funeral. The snow had started to fall again, soft and gentle, wrapping Winter Hollow in a blanket of white. The streets were quieter than usual, as the townspeople went about their business with heavy hearts, their minds still wrapped around the news of the sudden loss of their beloved Secret Santa. No one had expected him to pass away so abruptly, least of all in the middle of the holiday season. Yet, life had continued, almost too quickly, with the Christmas tree still standing in the town square, lights blinking cheerfully against the gray sky. The whole town was caught in an odd mix of mourning and holiday cheer, unsure of how to move forward without their holiday tradition.

And then, there was the gift.

It had arrived with a soft thud on the doorstep of the town hall, right on time, as though it had been waiting there all along. Wrapped in sparkling silver paper, tied with a simple red ribbon, it was unlike anything the town had ever received. Inside, beneath the wrapping, was an antique ornament. Beautiful, delicate, and unexpected, with intricate details that seemed to tell a story. The ornament sparkled faintly in the dimly lit room where it was now carefully placed on a table by the mayor's office.

Catherine Clarke, the town's librarian and a longtime friend of the late Secret Santa, had found herself the reluctant keeper of the gift. She had been there when the parcel arrived. She had been there when the first questions started swirling around. Who was it for? What did it mean? And most importantly—why had the Secret Santa chosen now, of all times, to send this final message? There was something almost otherworldly about the object. Something that seemed too perfect, too intentional. Catherine couldn't quite shake the feeling that the ornament held the key to something much bigger than just a holiday tradition.

It was late afternoon when Catherine sat alone in the town hall, holding the ornament in her hands, carefully turning it over to examine its craftsmanship. The ornament was in the shape of a bird, its wings spread wide as though ready to take flight. The wings were painted in a soft, iridescent blue, with delicate gold streaks running through the edges, giving it a look as if it had caught the first light of dawn. The bird's body was a deep crimson, almost as if it had been bathed in the glow of a setting sun. What struck Catherine the most were the tiny markings etched along the bird's side. At first glance, they looked like random lines, but upon closer inspection, she saw they formed a small message, barely noticeable, hidden in the folds of the ornament's design.

Her fingers brushed over the markings, tracing them carefully. The lines formed words, though in a language Catherine didn't recognize. Her heart began to race. Was this some kind of code? An ancient language? The mystery deepened with every moment she studied it, her mind spinning with possibilities.

Catherine stood up abruptly, the ornament still in her hands, and moved toward the small desk in the corner of the room where the town's records were kept. She flipped through the dusty books and papers, searching for anything that could give her a clue about the ornament's origins. Her eyes scanned each page in a hurry, flipping past family trees, old maps, and forgotten letters. And then, on the very last page of an old journal tucked in the back of a drawer, she found it. The name of the ornament's maker—an artisan from the town's early days.

The artisan was long gone, but the journal spoke of a tradition that had been lost to time—one that seemed to mirror the very essence of Winter Hollow. The ornament was not just a piece of decoration; it was a symbol. A symbol of new beginnings, of hopes for a brighter future, and most importantly, of redemption.

Catherine read the words aloud under her breath, trying to make sense of the passage. "This ornament is meant to remind the bearer that the past does not have to define them. Each new season brings with it the possibility for change." She paused, feeling a chill run down her spine. Could this be what the Secret Santa had been trying to convey? Could the ornament be pointing to a deeper meaning? The message felt like a key, a clue that would unlock something buried in the town's history, something no one had ever thought to look for.

With trembling hands, Catherine walked back to the ornament, holding it up to the light. The gold streaks shimmered, as if the ornament itself was trying to reveal its secrets. She closed her eyes for a moment, letting the silence of the room wash over her. There was something profound about it, something that tugged at her heart.

When she opened her eyes, she saw the reflection of her own face in the ornament's surface. But something else was there too—something she hadn't noticed before. The bird's eyes, the small details she'd missed earlier, seemed to be staring back at her, as if the ornament was calling to her, urging her to understand.

Her thoughts raced as she turned the ornament in her hands once again. The markings, the message, the bird's eyes—all of it was starting to make sense. The Secret Santa hadn't just left behind a gift; they had left behind a message for someone, for the entire town. It wasn't about the holiday season. It wasn't about the gifts or the traditions. It was about the town itself. It was about forgiveness, second chances, and the power of community. The ornament was a reminder that Winter Hollow could start anew, that the townspeople could heal from the wounds of the past and build something better together.

Catherine stood still for a moment, reflecting on the past few days. The loss of the Secret Santa had cast a shadow over the town, but it had also brought people together. For the first time in years, old friends and neighbors were talking again, coming together to remember the good times they had shared, to heal, and to forgive. The ornament, with its subtle yet powerful message, was the final gift—a gift of hope.

But there was one more question. Who was the recipient? Who had the Secret Santa chosen to receive this final gift? Catherine turned the ornament over once more, scanning the markings, searching for more clues. And then, just as she was about to give up, she noticed something small etched at the very base of the bird's tail.

It was a name.

A name she recognized immediately.

It was hers.

The realization hit Catherine like a wave. She was the recipient. The Secret Santa had chosen her. But why? Why had the late Secret Santa chosen her to receive this final gift, this powerful symbol of renewal and hope? What was she meant to do with it?

Tears filled her eyes as she looked around the room, at the town, at the people she had known her whole life. Winter Hollow had been through so much, yet it had endured. The town was still standing, its heart still beating. And now, it was her turn to help lead it into a new chapter, to guide it towards healing and redemption.

As Catherine held the ornament close to her heart, she felt a sense of peace wash over her. She wasn't alone. She never had been. The town was with her, and together, they would unlock the secrets of the past, embrace the promise of the future, and carry the gift of the Secret Santa's last message forward into the new year.

Echoes of Christmas Past

The frost had settled over Winter Hollow, the kind of chill that crept into your bones and made you long for the warmth of a crackling fire. Christmas was just days away, and despite the ongoing search for the mysterious recipient of the late Secret Santa's final gift, there was an undeniable sense of peace hanging in the air. The streets were lined with twinkling lights, the scent of freshly baked pies and cookies wafted from every window, and the town square was abuzz with the holiday spirit. Yet, there was something different this year. The death of the Secret Santa, the town's beloved benefactor who had quietly brought joy to Winter Hollow for as long as anyone could remember, had left a gap in the hearts of many.

Among those most affected by the loss was Mildred "Millie" Calloway, an elderly woman who had lived in the town for nearly all her eighty-three years. Millie was one of the few remaining residents who had witnessed the town's history firsthand, and with her sharp mind, she had a wealth of memories to share—if one was patient enough to listen. That afternoon, as the townspeople bustled about preparing for the festive celebrations, Millie sat on her porch, wrapped in a woolen shawl, a mug of hot cocoa cradled in her hands.

A young woman named Clara, eager to learn more about the history of Winter Hollow and its mysterious traditions, stopped by Millie's house. Clara had been particularly interested in the origins of the Secret Santa tradition, and Millie, being one of the oldest residents, was undoubtedly the best person to ask. She had lived through the town's ups and downs, and though she wasn't an obvious storyteller, Clara had heard whispers of stories that only Millie could tell.

"Good afternoon, Millie," Clara greeted, her breath forming a small cloud in the cold air. "I hope I'm not disturbing you."

Millie looked up, her sharp, blue eyes scanning Clara as if she were sizing her up. After a long pause, she finally smiled.

"No, child. Not at all. What brings you to my doorstep on this fine winter's day?"

Clara hesitated, feeling a bit uncertain. "I've been trying to understand more about the town's traditions—especially the Secret Santa. I heard you were around when it all started."

Millie chuckled softly, her gaze drifting toward the distant mountains that stood tall against the sky. "Ah, the Secret Santa... yes, I suppose you could say I was there when it began. But there's more to the story than you might think. Some things people forget over time. But I remember. I remember it all."

Clara's curiosity piqued. "Could you tell me about it?"

Millie leaned back in her rocking chair, the wood creaking softly beneath her. She took a slow sip from her mug, and after a moment, her eyes narrowed as if she were searching for the right words. "Well now, it was many years ago, back when this town was still young. I was just a girl, not much older than you. People didn't have much back then, but we had each other. Christmas was always special, but it wasn't always as grand as it is now. We didn't have these fancy lights or the big parties. We were a modest bunch, mostly farmers and shopkeepers, scraping by as best as we could."

She paused for a moment, her voice lowering as if she were lost in the memory. "But then came the winter of '56. It was one of the coldest winters we'd ever had, and I remember it like it was yesterday. The snow fell so thick that it covered the town in a blanket of white, and for weeks, no one could get in or out. The roads were impassable, and the cold seeped into every crack and crevice. It was so bad, we didn't even know if the postman was going to make it to deliver the letters."

Clara leaned forward, captivated. "That must have been difficult."

"It was," Millie agreed, her voice growing softer. "But what made it worse was that people were struggling. There wasn't enough food to go around. The winter crops had failed, and the local stores couldn't stock up quickly enough. The whole town was on the brink of desperation. People were looking for any way to keep their spirits up, and Christmas that year seemed like it might be a bleak one."

Clara could sense the sadness in Millie's words, but she also felt the hint of something more—a glimmer of hope that was yet to be revealed.

"And then," Millie continued, "just when it seemed like all was lost, a miracle happened. One by one, packages began appearing on doorsteps. No one knew who was leaving them, but they were filled with food, blankets, and little treats—things that people hadn't been able to afford. The mystery gifts arrived every day leading up to Christmas, and though the town was cold and struggling, those gifts brought warmth to our hearts. It didn't matter who sent them. What mattered was that someone cared."

Clara's heart fluttered as she listened. She had heard rumors about Winter Hollow's Secret Santa, but to hear it from someone who had lived through it made the story come alive.

"I don't understand," Clara said, her brow furrowed in confusion. "If no one knew who sent the gifts, how did the tradition begin?"

Millie smiled wistfully, a faraway look in her eyes. "Ah, that's where things get interesting. You see, those gifts weren't just from any one person. They came from a group of townsfolk—people who were in a better position to help, but who didn't want anyone to know. They believed in the spirit of Christmas, of community, and of giving without expecting anything in return. But there was one particular gift that stood out. It was left at the doorstep of old Eleanor Carver, who lived on the edge of town. She had a daughter who was very ill, and no one knew how they were going to make it through the winter. The gift was small—just a box with a note attached. And it read: 'For Eleanor, in her time of need. Merry Christmas from your Secret Santa.'"

Millie paused again, taking another sip of her cocoa. Clara waited, sensing there was more to the story.

"The thing is, Eleanor never told anyone about the gift," Millie continued. "She was proud, you see, and didn't want people to know she needed help. But that gift changed everything for her. She later told me that it gave her the strength to keep going, to keep fighting for her daughter. And she wasn't the only one. There were countless others who received help in secret."

Clara's mind raced as she processed the information. She had always thought the Secret Santa tradition was something that had started more recently, but now, it seemed like it had deep roots in the town's history. She was beginning to understand that the tradition wasn't just about giving—it was about preserving the town's sense of community and caring for one another.

"So, the Secret Santa wasn't just one person?" Clara asked, her voice filled with wonder.

Millie nodded slowly. "No, it was a group of people who came together every year, anonymously giving to those in need. Over time, they created the tradition that became what we know today—the Secret Santa. But what most people don't realize is that it wasn't always just about the gifts. It was about building bonds, about helping those who needed it the most, even when it wasn't obvious. Those gifts were a symbol of hope during dark times."

Clara sat in silence, her mind swirling with the revelations Millie had shared. The pieces of the puzzle were starting to come together. The mystery of the final gift—the one left behind by the late Secret Santa—wasn't just about the present itself. It was a culmination of the years of giving, of the town's hidden acts of kindness and love. The real gift wasn't material; it was the spirit of community, of helping one another in times of need.

"Thank you for sharing this with me," Clara said softly. "I had no idea the tradition went so far back."

Millie smiled warmly. "Most don't. But now you know. And I hope you'll carry that story with you. It's important, especially now."

As Clara stood to leave, she felt a renewed sense of purpose. The town's traditions were far deeper than she had imagined, and she could sense that this Christmas, the mystery surrounding the Secret Santa's final gift was more than just a passing curiosity. It was part of the town's legacy, a legacy that bound everyone together, no matter how much time had passed.

As the winter wind blew gently through the trees, Clara walked away from Millie's porch, her heart filled with the warmth of understanding. And as the snowflakes danced in the air, she couldn't help but wonder: Who was the recipient of the final gift, and what secret did it hold?

The Pine Tree Paradox

S now crunched beneath heavy boots as the townspeople of Winter Hollow gathered once again near the towering pine tree in the town square. The tree stood like a sentinel, its branches dusted with a delicate frosting of snow. This was no ordinary pine; it had been planted decades ago by the late Secret Santa himself, a man whose kindness had woven an unbreakable thread through the fabric of the town. In light of the recent discovery of his mysterious final gift, the tree had taken on an almost mythical quality. It was not merely a festive decoration but a living symbol of his enduring legacy. And now, whispers filled the air—the pine held a secret that might unravel the puzzle left behind.

Mary Clearwater, the elderly woman whose recollection of an event from fifty years ago had reignited hope among the townsfolk, stood closest to the tree. Her frail hands trembled slightly, whether from the cold or the weight of memory. "This tree," she began, her voice carrying a reverent tone, "was planted during a winter much like this one. A bitter cold year when the town came together, just as we are now. But there was something unusual about that day, something I had forgotten until recently." Her words hung in the frosty air, drawing the crowd closer.

"What was unusual?" asked Greg Winslow, the town's carpenter, his brow furrowed with curiosity. He had always been skeptical of stories that seemed too good to be true but couldn't deny the intrigue surrounding this one.

Mary looked up at the tree, her gray eyes misty. "The Secret Santa planted this tree as part of the annual festival, but there was a peculiar urgency about it. I remember him instructing everyone to step back as he placed something in the soil. A small box, perhaps. He said it was a time capsule, something to remind the town of the spirit of giving."

The crowd murmured in unison, the word "time capsule" sparking a wave of excitement. It had been decades since the event Mary described, and none of the younger residents had ever heard such a tale. Even the older ones, now that they thought about it, couldn't recall the tree being anything more than a thoughtful gesture.

Tommy Bell, the enthusiastic teenage son of the local florist, practically bounced in place. "A time capsule under the tree? That's like a treasure hunt! We have to dig it up and see what's inside."

But Mayor Evelyn Granger raised a gloved hand to restore order. "Let's not be too hasty. If this story is true, then the capsule might be connected to the Secret Santa's final gift. We need to approach this carefully and with respect."

The crowd quieted as Evelyn's calm authority settled over them. It was agreed that they would investigate, but not before ensuring they wouldn't harm the tree or disrupt the square's beloved festive charm. Greg offered to lead the effort, promising to use his carpentry tools to gently probe the soil.

The next morning, a smaller group gathered around the tree. The snow was brushed away, revealing the sturdy base of the pine. Greg knelt and began digging with precision, the onlookers holding their breath as each handful of soil was removed. The work was slow, the tension palpable. Every scrape of the spade against the frozen ground seemed louder than it was.

Then came the moment. Greg paused, brushing away the last layer of dirt with his gloved hands. "I've found something," he announced, his voice tight with excitement. Carefully, he lifted a small wooden box from the ground. The wood was aged but remarkably intact, the lock rusted yet holding firm. The townspeople pressed closer, their faces a mix of awe and eagerness.

"Open it," someone urged, but Greg hesitated. "Let's bring it to the town hall. We should do this together, with everyone present."

By evening, the entire town had packed into the hall, their breath clouding the frosty air as they waited. The box sat on a table at the center of the room, a spotlight illuminating it like a holy relic. Evelyn, as the mayor, took the honor of attempting to open it. With a small effort, the lock gave way, and the lid creaked open, revealing its contents.

Inside was an envelope, yellowed with age, and a small wooden ornament carved into the shape of a star. The ornament gleamed faintly as if it had been polished regularly despite its time underground. Evelyn picked up the envelope, her hands steady but her expression unreadable. She unfolded the letter inside and began to read aloud:

"To the people of Winter Hollow,

If you're reading this, it means the time has come to remember what truly matters. This star is not just a decoration. It is a reminder that the brightest light comes from within each of you. The traditions we uphold, the kindness we share—these are what make our town special. But sometimes, we need a little nudge to see it clearly.

This tree was planted to grow alongside our community, its roots as deep as the bonds we form with one another. The star is meant for someone who embodies the spirit of giving, someone who will carry forward the legacy of bringing joy to others. Look around you and decide together who that person is. When you find them, give them this star, and they will know what to do next.

Yours faithfully, The Secret Santa"

The room was silent, save for the soft rustling of the letter as Evelyn folded it. The weight of the Secret Santa's words settled over everyone, their meaning both clear and enigmatic. The star was meant to be passed on, but to whom? And what would they be expected to do?

As the crowd dispersed, conversations buzzed. People speculated who among them might be chosen, their thoughts ranging from the obvious candidates—those who had always been generous—to the surprising ones, individuals whose quiet contributions had often gone unnoticed. In a town like Winter Hollow, everyone had their own idea of what giving truly meant.

Meanwhile, Evelyn held onto the star, unsure of how to proceed. The responsibility of interpreting the Secret Santa's intentions weighed heavily on her. She decided to consult with Mary, whose memories seemed to hold the key to so many parts of this mystery. Over tea that evening, Mary shared more about the Secret Santa's character—his knack for seeing potential in people, his unwavering belief in second chances. "He would want us to choose not just someone who gives, but someone who inspires others to give as well," Mary said thoughtfully.

Days passed, and the town seemed to grow closer in their quest to solve the Pine Tree Paradox. People began performing small acts of kindness, perhaps hoping to prove their worthiness for the star or simply inspired by the spirit of the season. The bakery offered free cookies, the florist gave away holly wreaths, and even the gruff mechanic at the garage surprised everyone by fixing cars free of charge.

One evening, as the snow fell softly outside, Evelyn stood in the square holding the star. The tree's lights twinkled above her, casting a warm glow over the gathering crowd. "After much thought," she began, "I believe the Secret Santa's message was not just about finding one person, but about reminding us all of the power of giving. However, there is someone among us who has shown us that power time and time again."

She turned to Mary, who looked stunned as the crowd erupted in applause. "Mary Clearwater, your stories and your wisdom have brought us together in ways we could never have imagined. This star belongs to you."

Tears streamed down Mary's cheeks as she accepted the star. "I don't know what to say," she whispered, her voice thick with emotion. "But I promise to honor this gift and the spirit of our Secret Santa."

As Mary held the star high, the town cheered, their voices ringing out like a joyful carol. The mystery of the Pine Tree

Paradox had been solved, but its message lingered, a reminder that the greatest gift of all was the love and kindness they shared. And under the watchful branches of the old pine, Winter Hollow felt more like home than ever before.

The Toy Maker's Tale

The gentle hum of the workshop filled the room, broken only by the soft creak of the wooden chair as old Mr. Whitaker leaned back, his gaze fixed on the tiny wooden train in his hands. For decades, he had crafted toys for the children of Winter Hollow, his creations known for their intricate details and timeless charm. Tonight, though, his hands trembled slightly as he ran a thumb along the freshly painted edges of the train. It was as if the little toy carried the weight of a memory too tender to hold and too powerful to forget.

The crowd gathered in the toy shop wasn't there for wooden trains or hand-carved dolls tonight. They had come for a story. After the revelation by the pine tree—its hollow trunk concealing an old journal with cryptic sketches and notes—the town had turned to Mr. Whitaker. His name was scrawled in the journal, along with a date from nearly five decades ago. What connection did the kindly toymaker have to the mysterious traditions of their dearly departed Secret Santa? And how could his tale bring them closer to unraveling the mystery of the last gift?

Mr. Whitaker had been reluctant at first. "Memories can be delicate things," he had murmured to the mayor, who had been the one to ask. But as he glanced around at the eager faces—young and old, all knit together by curiosity and the need for answers—he knew that some stories were meant to be shared, especially on a snowy evening in December.

Clearing his throat, Mr. Whitaker placed the train carefully on the counter and gestured for everyone to gather closer. The warmth of the fire in the corner mixed with the soft scent of sawdust and peppermint from a jar on the shelf. It was a scene that felt more like a story itself, something plucked straight from a Christmas card. "You're all wondering about the journal, aren't you?" he began, his voice rich and steady, each word steeped in years of wisdom.

The crowd nodded as if their collective anticipation could coax the tale out of him. Mr. Whitaker smiled faintly, folding his hands in his lap. "Well, it begins with a man you all loved and miss dearly—Samuel Everett, your Secret Santa."

A hushed murmur swept through the room. Samuel's name had become synonymous with warmth, generosity, and the unspoken magic of Winter Hollow. He had been the heart of their Christmases, yet so much of his life remained shrouded in mystery.

"Before he was your Secret Santa," Mr. Whitaker continued, "Samuel was a man searching for redemption. He came to this town carrying not only a battered suitcase but also the weight of choices he regretted. I met him on his first day here, right here in this shop." He gestured to the worn counter. "He was a traveler then, looking for work. I hired him to help me with the toys, though he'd never carved a thing in his life. What he lacked in skill, he made up for in spirit. He had this way about him—kind eyes, a quiet laugh, and a yearning to belong."

The toymaker paused, his own eyes clouded with the memories of that winter long ago. "One evening, after we'd closed up, Samuel stayed back. He had found a broken rocking horse in the corner and decided to fix it. I told him it wasn't worth the effort, but he just smiled and said, 'Every broken thing deserves a chance to be whole again.'"

The crowd leaned in closer as Mr. Whitaker's voice softened. "It wasn't long before Samuel told me why he'd come to Winter Hollow. He'd left behind a life of wealth and comfort, a life that he said had made him forget what truly mattered. He'd made mistakes—pushed people away, hurt those he cared for. But he'd found a kind of peace in this little town. And it was here that he had an idea, one that would shape all of our lives."

The toymaker picked up the wooden train again, turning it over in his hands as though it held the secret to the story. "It was Samuel who first proposed the idea of a Secret Santa gift exchange. He said that giving without expectation, without recognition, was the truest form of kindness. That first year, we kept it small—just a few families, a few modest gifts. Samuel insisted on handmaking his contribution, a small wooden star carved right here in this shop."

Mr. Whitaker paused as the memories washed over him. "The star went to a little girl whose father had lost his job. I'll never forget her face when she opened the package. It wasn't the gift itself that brought her joy; it was the thought behind it. Samuel told me later that her smile was the first time he'd truly felt at peace in years."

The toymaker glanced out the frost-covered window, where the snow was beginning to fall in thick, silent flakes.

"Year after year, Samuel carried on the tradition, and it grew into the Secret Santa exchange you all know. But there's something most of you don't know. Samuel's gifts—they weren't just random acts of kindness. They were his way of mending the broken things, the unseen cracks in people's lives. Each gift had a purpose, a message, a story."

The room was utterly silent now, save for the crackle of the fire. Even the youngest children, who usually fidgeted during long stories, sat wide-eyed and motionless.

"Now, about that journal," Mr. Whitaker said, his voice taking on a new weight. "The sketches in it—they were Samuel's plans. Ideas for gifts that he hoped would touch lives in ways no one else could. And there's one sketch in particular..." He reached beneath the counter and retrieved a yellowed page from a stack of papers. "This," he said, holding it up, "is the last design Samuel worked on before he passed. He called it his 'final gift.'"

The page depicted an ornate music box, its lid shaped like the pine tree that now stood at the center of the town square. "The pine tree," someone whispered, and Mr. Whitaker nodded.

"Yes," he said. "Samuel planted that tree himself the same year he started the Secret Santa tradition. He said it was a symbol of hope and resilience. I believe his final gift is tied to it, though I don't yet know how."

The room buzzed with speculation as people exchanged theories in hushed tones. But Mr. Whitaker wasn't finished. "Samuel often said that the greatest gifts weren't the ones you could hold in your hands, but the ones that stayed in your heart. Whatever his last gift is, I believe it's meant to remind us of that truth. And perhaps," he added, his gaze sweeping over the room, "it's meant to remind us of him."

As the townspeople left the shop that night, their minds spinning with questions and possibilities, Mr. Whitaker lingered by the fire. He picked up the little wooden train again, a wistful smile playing on his lips. In his heart, he knew that Samuel's final gift was more than a mystery to be solved—it was a lesson, a reminder of the magic that comes when a community comes together, bound by love, hope, and the spirit of giving.

Outside, the snow fell heavier, blanketing Winter Hollow in a soft, silvery glow. The pine tree in the square stood tall and proud, its branches whispering secrets only the wind could carry. Somewhere in its roots, or perhaps in the hearts of the people it watched over, Samuel Everett's legacy lived on.

A Melody in the Wind

In the heart of Winter Hollow, the snowfall that had begun with a delicate dusting earlier in the day had now grown into a soft, swirling cascade. The town's streets shimmered under the glow of festive lights, their reflection painting the frosted shop windows with golden hues. The toymaker's tale, told in the warmth of his little shop, had left a hush among those who heard it. People now regarded the legacy of the Secret Santa not just as an annual tradition, but as a piece of their own hearts—a reflection of kindness that bound the community together.

As the evening deepened, the toymaker stood in his quiet workshop. The story he had shared earlier about the inspiration for the Secret Santa—the simple act of generosity from a stranger that had transformed his life—lingered in his thoughts. He wiped his glasses and sighed, gazing at the array of unfinished toys, each one imbued with his labor of love. His fingers brushed a forgotten corner of his workbench, where something odd caught his attention.

Hidden beneath a layer of wood shavings and an old cloth lay a small box, its surface carved with delicate, swirling patterns. He paused, feeling a strange tug in his chest. This was no ordinary box. The craftsmanship was finer than anything he remembered making, its surface gleaming even in the dim light of the workshop. Lifting it gently, he noticed a faint inscription at the base, almost invisible to the naked eye: *To Winter Hollow, with love.*

Curiosity prickled his mind. He turned the tiny key protruding from the side of the box, and the room was instantly filled with the hauntingly beautiful notes of a melody. The tune was unfamiliar yet deeply moving, a combination of joy and longing that made him close his eyes. The music seemed alive, wrapping the space in a gentle embrace. He wasn't alone in the workshop anymore—at least, it didn't feel like it.

Word spread quickly about the discovery of the music box. The next morning, a small group of townsfolk gathered in the toymaker's shop. They stood around the box, their expressions ranging from awe to puzzlement as the melody played once again. Each person felt something different in its tune: a bittersweet memory, a comforting warmth, or an unexplainable yearning. It was as if the music spoke directly to their souls, carrying a message that words could never convey.

The mayor, a sturdy man with a booming voice, stepped forward. "This must be part of the Secret Santa's final gift," he declared, his tone decisive yet tinged with wonder. "We need to understand what this means. Perhaps it's a clue, something to guide us to the next piece of the puzzle."

Among the crowd, young Clara—a schoolteacher known for her sharp mind and gentle heart—spoke up. "The melody feels familiar, like something I've heard before. Could it be connected to the town's history?" Her suggestion stirred murmurs of agreement. Winter Hollow was rich in traditions, many of which had faded with time.

Encouraged by the idea, the group decided to dig deeper into the melody's origins. They combed through old records in the town's archives, a dusty corner of the library seldom visited except during historical festivals. Clara and the toymaker worked side by side, poring over faded music sheets and brittle newspaper clippings.

Days passed, and the music box continued to play its enigmatic tune. Children hummed it as they built snowmen, shopkeepers whistled it while arranging their Christmas displays, and even the church bells seemed to echo its rhythm. The melody had woven itself into the fabric of Winter Hollow, becoming as much a part of the season as the wreaths and garlands that adorned every door.

One evening, Clara stumbled upon a journal in the archives. It belonged to Margaret Blythe, the town's first music teacher, who had passed away nearly a century ago. The pages were filled with handwritten compositions, and among them was a piece titled *A Melody in the Wind*. Clara's heart raced as she realized the notes matched those of the music box. But there was more—Margaret had written a note beneath the composition: *For those who seek the spirit of giving, let this tune be a guide.*

The discovery added a new layer to the mystery. Margaret Blythe had been known for her generosity, often teaching children music lessons for free and organizing charity concerts to support struggling families. Could it be that her spirit had somehow influenced the Secret Santa tradition?

Back in the toymaker's workshop, the group gathered once more to discuss their findings. The room was filled with the scent of pine and the glow of a crackling fire. Clara placed the journal on the table, its open pages revealing the original composition. The melody began to feel less like an enigma and more like a bridge—a connection between the past and the present, between Margaret's legacy and the Secret Santa's mission.

But one question remained unanswered: Who was the recipient of the final gift? And why had the music box been left for the town to find?

As if in response to their unspoken thoughts, a gust of wind swept through the workshop, rustling the pages of the journal. The music box, which had been silent for a while, began to play again. This time, the melody seemed to change slightly, introducing a new note—a higher, lighter sound that hadn't been there before. The group exchanged glances, a mixture of astonishment and apprehension.

"Maybe the answer isn't in the past," the toymaker said softly. "Maybe it's right here, in this room, in what we choose to do next." His words carried weight, reminding everyone that the true essence of the Secret Santa was not just in uncovering a mystery but in embracing the spirit of giving.

The town rallied together, inspired by the melody and its message. They organized a special event—a concert in honor of Margaret Blythe and the Secret Santa. On Christmas Eve, the entire community gathered in the town square, where a makeshift stage had been set up. The music box took center stage, its haunting tune accompanied by musicians playing violins, flutes, and guitars.

As the final notes of the melody filled the air, a sense of peace settled over Winter Hollow. People hugged, laughed, and shared stories, their hearts lighter than they had been in years. The toymaker, standing at the edge of the crowd, felt a tear slip down his cheek. He realized that the gift wasn't just the music box or the mystery it carried—it was the way it had brought the town together, reminding them of the power of generosity and the beauty of connection.

And as the snow continued to fall, covering the town in a blanket of white, the wind carried the melody far beyond Winter Hollow, as if spreading its message to the world: The spirit of giving is the greatest gift of all.

The Star of Winter Hollow

The clock tower bells chimed faintly through the snow-laden air, their echoes blending with the distant hum of carolers. Winter Hollow, now buzzing with the mystery of the late Secret Santa's final gift, was wrapped in a palpable mix of anticipation and warmth. The discovery of the music box had left the town on edge, its haunting melody stirring something unnameable in each person who heard it. For some, it awakened bittersweet memories; for others, it was a call to action, a reminder of unfinished stories waiting to be told. But none could have predicted that the next piece of the puzzle would reveal itself not in a whisper, but in a dazzling burst of light.

It was young Lily Hart who stumbled upon the Christmas star. Lily, a curious girl of twelve with an eye for details most missed, had wandered into the town hall's attic on a whim. The music box had been placed there temporarily for safekeeping, its tune still lingering in the minds of all who'd heard it. Lily, unable to resist her curiosity, had snuck up the creaky stairs, her lantern casting playful shadows on the cobwebbed walls. As she approached the music box, something else caught her eye: a wooden crate pushed haphazardly into the corner, partially hidden under an old quilt. Tugging at the quilt, she uncovered a weathered box, marked with the faint inscription: "The Star of Winter Hollow."

Inside, nestled in a bed of soft velvet, lay an ornate Christmas star. It was unlike anything Lily had ever seen, its craftsmanship so intricate that it seemed alive. Golden rays spiraled outwards, interwoven with tiny, glittering gemstones that sparkled even in the dim light of the attic. At the center of the star was a translucent crystal, etched with delicate carvings that resembled the very streets and homes of Winter Hollow. Lily's heart raced as she reached out to touch it, feeling a warmth emanating from the object, as though it carried the essence of the town itself. Unable to contain her excitement, she hurried downstairs to show the others.

Word of Lily's discovery spread faster than the morning frost. By midday, nearly the entire town had gathered in the square, huddled together under scarves and coats. The star was placed atop the grand fountain, where the late Secret Santa had often been seen during his quiet moments of reflection. The mayor, a pragmatic yet deeply sentimental man, addressed the crowd, his voice steady despite the chill. "This star," he began, "is more than a decoration. It is a message, a piece of a larger story that our Secret Santa has left behind. A story we must uncover together."

As the star's light caught the setting sun, a soft hum filled the air, resonating with the same haunting melody of the music box. Gasps rippled through the crowd as the crystal at the star's center began to glow, projecting a delicate map onto the snow-dusted ground. It was a map of Winter Hollow, but not as it stood today. The map revealed an older version of the town, its streets winding differently, its landmarks slightly altered. At the edge of the projection was a small, flickering light, as if beckoning the townsfolk to follow.

Among the gathered crowd stood Eleanor Frost, the town librarian and an unspoken keeper of its history. Eleanor had been unusually quiet since the discovery of the music box, her mind racing with connections and possibilities. Now, as she gazed at the map, something clicked. She stepped forward, her voice clear and deliberate. "That light marks the old starlight trail," she said. "It's a path that hasn't been used in decades. My grandmother used to tell me stories about it—a place where wishes were made, where people went to find hope."

A murmur spread through the crowd, a mixture of excitement and apprehension. The starlight trail was shrouded in legend, its exact location lost to time and overgrowth. But now, with the star's map as their guide, it seemed as though the path was calling them back. Determined not to let the moment slip away, a small group of volunteers, led by Eleanor, set out to follow the trail, the glowing map their only guide. Lily, clutching her lantern tightly, insisted on joining them, her youthful curiosity outweighing the cold.

The journey to the starlight trail was both eerie and enchanting. The snow seemed to muffle every sound except the crunch of their boots and the occasional rustle of wind through the trees. The star's light guided them through thickets and across frozen streams, illuminating a path that felt both familiar and otherworldly. Along the way, the group shared stories—tales of the Secret Santa's kindness, of the lives he'd touched and the quiet joy he'd brought to Winter Hollow. Each story seemed to weave itself into the fabric of the trail, as though the path itself were listening.

Finally, they reached a clearing. In the center stood an ancient tree, its branches bare but adorned with strings of weathered bells and ornaments. At its base was a stone pedestal, upon which sat a leather-bound journal. Eleanor approached it cautiously, brushing off the snow to reveal the inscription on the cover: "To the Heart of Winter Hollow." Opening the journal, she began to read aloud, her voice trembling with emotion.

The journal was a letter from the Secret Santa, written as though he had known this moment would come. In it, he spoke of his love for the town and its people, of his belief in the power of kindness and community. He revealed that the star was more than a family heirloom; it was a symbol of hope, passed down through generations. His final wish was for the town to come together, to rediscover the starlight trail not as individuals, but as a united community. "The star shines brightest," he wrote, "when its light is shared."

Tears streamed down faces as Eleanor's voice carried through the clearing. The group returned to the town square, carrying the journal and the star with a newfound sense of purpose. That evening, the star was placed atop the town's Christmas tree, its light casting a warm, golden glow over Winter Hollow. The townsfolk gathered beneath it, their voices rising in song as they held hands and shared stories of the Secret Santa's legacy.

In the days that followed, the spirit of the starlight trail seemed to infuse every corner of the town. Old feuds were mended, neighbors reached out to one another, and the sense of community that had once defined Winter Hollow was rekindled. The star became a symbol not just of the Secret

Santa's final gift, but of the enduring power of love, hope, and togetherness.

As the snow continued to fall, blanketing the town in a soft hush, Lily looked up at the glowing star and smiled. She didn't know what the future held, but she knew one thing for certain: the light of Winter Hollow would never fade, as long as its people held it in their hearts. And somewhere, in the quiet stillness of the night, the Secret Santa's spirit seemed to linger, a gentle reminder that the greatest gifts are the ones we give to each other.

Midnight at the Clock Tower

The chill of the winter night wrapped itself around the small town of Winter Hollow like a blanket, thick and comforting, yet carrying with it the unmistakable bite of December's late-night air. The streets, usually quiet at this hour, were filled with a kind of buzz, an electric energy that seemed to hum beneath the surface of every conversation, every footstep. Tonight was different. Tonight was something the townspeople would remember for years to come. Tonight, they would discover the final secret of their beloved Secret Santa.

The clock tower in the center of town stood tall, its silhouette framed against the sky, the faint glow of a thousand Christmas lights twinkling across the rooftops below. In just a few moments, the bell would toll midnight, and with it, the final mystery would be revealed. For weeks now, the town had been buzzing with questions. Who would the last gift go to? What could possibly be inside the final package? And more than anything, who had their beloved Secret Santa truly been?

It had all started weeks ago, when the townspeople had received their annual gift from the elusive Secret Santa—small tokens of kindness, personalized just for each recipient. Some had received books, others cozy scarves, and a few even small, hand-painted ornaments. The gifts always appeared mysteriously, often on doorsteps, sometimes hanging from lampposts. No one ever knew who the Secret Santa was, but everyone had their own theories. But this year, everything changed when news of the Secret Santa's sudden passing spread through the town like wildfire.

The gift-giving had stopped, but the promise of one final present had lingered, left unfinished. It had remained a source of quiet conversation—who would be the lucky recipient? Who deserved this final act of kindness? And what was inside that last mysterious box, sealed with the red ribbon, sitting in the center of the town square, beneath the shadow of the clock tower?

The air had grown colder as the clock ticked toward midnight, and a gathering had slowly formed in the square, its members standing close together for warmth and companionship. Some of the older residents had wrapped themselves in thick coats and scarves, while the younger ones, eager to finally uncover the mystery, stood on tiptoe, their faces lit with a mix of anticipation and excitement. The small square had been decorated with holly and ivy, the streets lined with glowing lanterns, casting a soft, golden light over the crowd that had gathered to witness the unveiling. In a town known for its quiet, simple charm, there was an undeniable sense of occasion in the air tonight.

Among the crowd was Grace Williams, a local schoolteacher whose gentle spirit and kind heart had made her beloved in the town. Her hands were tucked into the pockets of her woolen coat, her breath visible in the crisp night air. She glanced around at the faces she had known all her life, their expressions a mix of wonder, anxiety, and curiosity. She, too, had wondered about the gift. She had seen the package placed on the pedestal earlier in the evening—a small, beautifully wrapped box, no larger than a shoebox, sitting quietly beneath the glow of a nearby lantern. A note, written in the same flowing script as all the previous year's gifts, had been attached: *"For someone who believes in magic."*

Her heart had fluttered when she read the words. Magic. Was that a clue? Was she the recipient? Or was it someone else? And yet, no one knew. No one dared to guess. There had been hushed conversations, a few wagers, and even some speculation, but nothing concrete. The mystery had become something almost sacred. The town's collective heart beat faster as the bell tower's hands inched closer to twelve.

At the back of the square, near the steps of the clock tower, stood Ethan Carter, the town's sheriff, his face hard to read beneath the brim of his dark hat. Ethan had known the late Secret Santa well—an older man who had lived a quiet, simple life in the town. He had been one of the first to discover the unexpected death, and in the weeks that followed, he had tried, with all his might, to shield the townspeople from the grief of losing someone so integral to their lives. But it had been impossible. The Secret Santa had been a beacon of warmth, of generosity, a thread that connected everyone in Winter Hollow. And now, he was gone.

But as Ethan looked out at the crowd tonight, he couldn't help but feel the weight of a secret he had kept. He knew the identity of the final recipient of the gift. He had known all along. The only question was whether or not they would be ready for the truth. It wasn't just about the gift—it was about everything that had led up to this moment. The town's heart had been broken, yes, but it would heal in the strangest of ways.

The bell tower struck one, its deep chimes reverberating across the town, filling the square with a sense of finality. The crowd grew silent, their breath coming in shallow gasps as they waited. The air seemed to crackle with a thousand unspoken words, a thousand questions that would finally be answered.

Grace held her breath. Her eyes flicked to the pedestal, to the little gift. Would it change everything for her? For the town?

As the bell struck its final toll, a hush fell over Winter Hollow, broken only by the sound of footsteps in the snow. Ethan moved forward, his hands steady as he approached the gift. The small crowd parted as he made his way to the pedestal, and for a moment, everything seemed to stop—time, the night, the world itself—frozen in anticipation.

Ethan reached for the box, lifting it gently, carefully, as if it held not just a gift, but something more. Something priceless. He turned slowly to face the crowd, and a murmur rippled through the group. He cleared his throat.

"Winter Hollow," he began, his voice carrying the weight of the moment. "We all know that our beloved Secret Santa has passed away. And tonight, we are gathered here for one last gift. But this... this gift is more than just a gesture. It is the heart of this town. And so, it belongs to someone who has touched all of us, in one way or another."

Ethan's eyes scanned the crowd. For a moment, no one moved. Everyone seemed to be holding their breath, as if they had all been waiting for this very moment, this revelation.

Grace stood frozen, her heart racing. Could it be her?

Ethan continued. "This gift, this final act of kindness, is for someone who has always believed in the power of community.

Someone who knows the magic of bringing people together. This gift is for the person who, despite their own struggles, has always shown up for others. And that person is—"

He paused, letting the moment linger in the cold night air. The crowd leaned in.

"This gift is for Grace Williams."

Gasps rippled through the crowd. Grace's hand flew to her chest as she stared at Ethan, disbelief flooding her veins. How could it be her? She had done nothing special. Nothing extraordinary. She was just a simple teacher, living her quiet life.

Ethan stepped forward, handing her the box. "You've touched this town more than you know, Grace. And tonight, the Secret Santa wanted you to have the last gift."

Tears welled in Grace's eyes as she took the box. The crowd was silent, waiting for her to open it. She carefully untied the ribbon, and the soft paper fell away, revealing a small, delicate wooden ornament—a star, intricately carved with a message.

"May you always find your way back to the light."

Grace's breath caught in her throat. It was the same message she had written in a letter to the Secret Santa years ago, when she had first moved to Winter Hollow. She had written about finding her way through the darkness, about finding hope again after losing her parents. She had never expected the letter to be answered. But it had been, in the most beautiful way imaginable.

The town stood in awe as Grace held the ornament close to her chest, her heart swelling with gratitude. This wasn't just a gift. It was a message. A reminder that even in the darkest times, there was always light, always hope, always love. And with that, the mystery of the Secret Santa was complete. The final gift had been given. And in the glow of the Christmas lights, Winter Hollow would forever carry the warmth of that kindness, for as long as the town stood.

The Gift of Forgiveness

As the clock struck midnight, the tiny town of Winter Hollow glowed under a blanket of snow. Christmas Eve had come and gone, but the holiday spirit still lingered in the hearts of the townspeople. Inside the town hall, a gathering of residents buzzed with nervous energy, excitement, and a shared sense of wonder. The mysterious final gift from the late Secret Santa had yet to be revealed, and everyone was on edge, wondering who the recipient was and what the gift would mean for them.

For weeks now, the town had been consumed with speculation. Who was it for? What did it symbolize? The cryptic clues left behind by the late Secret Santa seemed to point toward something deeper than just a present. Some whispered that the gift was meant to mend broken relationships, others believed it was a symbol of redemption, but no one knew for sure.

In the corner of the room stood Margaret, the town's beloved postmistress. She had known the late Secret Santa longer than most. As the one who had received the gifts each year, sorted the cards, and kept the secret safe, she had always felt a special connection to the man who brought so much joy to Winter Hollow. Now, as she gazed around the room, she saw familiar faces—faces that had grown accustomed to the small town's ways. Yet there was an undercurrent of sadness in the air. The absence of the Secret Santa was palpable.

Margaret stood silently, her heart heavy with a mixture of emotions. She had promised herself she would keep the truth hidden, but as the town eagerly awaited the unveiling of the final gift, she knew the time had come. It was time to honor the wishes of the late Secret Santa, and perhaps, just perhaps, it was time to heal some old wounds.

The room quieted as the town's mayor, a stout man with a bushy mustache, stood at the front of the hall. His voice was steady, though there was a trace of emotion in it that he tried to mask. "Thank you all for being here tonight," he said. "We gather together not only to celebrate Christmas but to honor the spirit of giving that our dear friend, the Secret Santa, brought to all of us. His passing has left a void in this town, one that will be felt for years to come. But before we bid him farewell, we have one last gift to reveal—a gift that was left behind for someone in this room. We are here tonight to find out who that someone is."

The crowd shifted, their eyes widening with anticipation. Margaret felt a pang in her chest. She had been entrusted with the knowledge of who the recipient was, but she wasn't sure she was ready to share it. The story behind the gift was personal, intimate even, and it had the power to change things forever.

A hush fell over the room as the mayor reached for the large, intricately wrapped box that sat on the table. The box was simple in its design, but there was something about it that felt sacred, almost like it contained the weight of a thousand unspoken words. The mayor carefully unwrapped it, revealing a small, velvet pouch tied with a delicate ribbon. He paused, looking around at the gathered crowd. "Inside this pouch," he began, "is a letter. A letter from our Secret Santa."

He took a deep breath, then slowly opened the pouch and pulled out a folded piece of parchment. The letter, yellowed with age, had the unmistakable scent of ink and old paper. Margaret held her breath, knowing that the words contained within it would change everything.

The mayor cleared his throat and began to read aloud.

"To the recipient of my final gift,

By the time you read this, I will no longer be among you. But before I leave, I want to offer you one last gift—one that I hope will bring healing, peace, and forgiveness.

You and I, we have a history, one that is far from perfect. There have been misunderstandings, hurtful words, and regrets. But I've come to realize that life is too short to hold on to grudges, too short to let bitterness fester. The gift I leave you is not wrapped in bright paper or tied with a bow, but it is one that will last far longer than anything material.

I ask for your forgiveness. Not for the mistakes I made, but for the ones I allowed to go unspoken. For the love that I didn't give, and for the kindness I withheld. Please know that I have always loved you, even when I didn't know how to show it. This gift is my way of making amends, of offering you a chance to let go of the past and embrace the future with an open heart.

I hope that one day, you will see this not as a gift, but as the closure we both needed.

With love,

Your Secret Santa"

A murmur spread through the crowd as the mayor finished reading the letter. There was a collective gasp, a sense of disbelief. For many, the letter was more than just words on a page—it was a revelation. It spoke of regret, of a bond broken long ago, of unhealed wounds that had festered in the quiet corners of the town. And now, the town waited to find out who the recipient of this final, heartfelt gift was.

Margaret knew, of course. She had known all along. The letter had been written for someone who had once been a part of the Secret Santa's life, someone whose pain had remained buried beneath layers of time and silence. The recipient was someone the town had long forgotten—someone whose story had been overshadowed by the bright lights of the festive season.

Margaret's eyes moved slowly across the room, stopping at one figure in particular. It was Olivia, the town's librarian. Olivia had been a close friend of the Secret Santa years ago, but something had driven a wedge between them. There had been rumors, whispers of a falling out, but no one knew the full story. Olivia had never spoken of it, and over time, she had become somewhat of a recluse. Yet, through all the years, the Secret Santa had never stopped watching over her, never stopped caring.

As the crowd waited in silence, the mayor turned to Olivia, his face soft with understanding. "Olivia," he said, his voice gentle, "the final gift is for you."

The room fell still. Olivia's eyes widened in shock, and for a moment, she looked as if she might collapse. She had no idea this was coming. She had not expected to be the recipient of the Secret Santa's last gift, and certainly not in this way.

Margaret stepped forward, her heart heavy with emotion. She walked up to Olivia, placing a comforting hand on her shoulder. Olivia looked up at her, tears welling in her eyes.

"I know," Margaret whispered, "I know. It's time."

Olivia nodded, slowly unwrapping the velvet pouch. Inside, she found another letter, this one written in the familiar, loving handwriting of the Secret Santa. With trembling hands, she unfolded it and read aloud.

"I've always believed in the power of forgiveness, Olivia. And now, I hope you'll believe in it too. You've carried the weight of my mistakes for far too long. It's time for us to both be free from the past, to heal, and to move forward. Forgiveness is the greatest gift we can give ourselves. I hope you'll find peace in this final message, and know that I've always loved you, even when I didn't know how to show it.

With all my heart,

Your Secret Santa"

The room was silent for a long moment as Olivia folded the letter, wiping away a tear. She looked up at the gathered townspeople, her eyes filled with a mix of sadness and relief.

"I forgive you," she whispered, her voice barely audible, but the weight of the words was immense. "I've carried this pain for far too long, and it's time to let it go."

As the townspeople applauded, a wave of peace seemed to wash over Winter Hollow. The mystery was solved, the wounds were healed, and the gift of forgiveness had finally been received. In that moment, the town realized that the true magic of Christmas wasn't in the presents or the decorations—it was in the ability to forgive, to let go of the past, and to move forward with love and grace.

And so, the final gift was given. Not wrapped in paper, but in the form of redemption, healing, and the chance to start anew. The legacy of the Secret Santa lived on, not in the gifts he had given, but in the hearts he had touched, and in the bonds he had helped to restore.

As the clock struck one, the town of Winter Hollow gathered together, united in a moment of peace and joy, knowing that the true spirit of Christmas had been restored, not through gifts, but through the healing power of forgiveness.

A Starry Christmas Eve

As the evening sky deepened into a blanket of midnight blue, the town of Winter Hollow was a vision of serene Christmas beauty. Snowflakes drifted lazily from the heavens, settling gently on rooftops, trees, and the streets below. The scent of pine and cinnamon lingered in the crisp winter air. The Christmas lights twinkled on every house, casting a warm, festive glow over the quiet town square. It was Christmas Eve, the night the community had been waiting for—the night they would gather in the town square to honor the memory of their beloved Secret Santa.

The town had never been the same since the passing of the Secret Santa. The mysterious figure had been a part of Winter Hollow for as long as anyone could remember, leaving behind anonymous gifts, small tokens of kindness that brightened even the coldest of winters. But now, with the death of the Secret Santa, the spirit of the town seemed to waver. The gifts had stopped coming, and the magic of the holidays felt dimmer than it ever had before. The loss of their cherished gift-bringer was felt by everyone, but what had begun as sorrow soon turned to an urgent determination.

Tonight, on this starry Christmas Eve, the community had come together to honor the Secret Santa's legacy. The town hall had been decorated with garlands of evergreen and twinkling lights, a giant Christmas tree standing tall in the center. Beneath the tree, where once there had been nothing but empty space, stood a small wooden table adorned with a single chair. On the table rested the final gift from the Secret Santa—a wrapped box, old and slightly worn, with a red ribbon tied neatly around it. It had been placed there by the family of the late Secret Santa, but no one knew what was inside. The mystery had consumed the town for weeks, the anticipation growing with each passing day.

The clock struck midnight, and the crowd gathered in the square, their faces illuminated by the soft light of the Christmas decorations. The air was filled with a quiet hum of conversation, but there was also a reverence, a collective breath being held in anticipation of what would happen next.

At the front of the gathering stood Abigail, the town's mayor, her face set with determination. She was the one who had organized this ceremony, a way to bring closure to the mystery of the Secret Santa's last gift. In her hands, she held a small piece of parchment. Her voice, when she spoke, was steady and strong, carrying through the silent square like a beacon.

"Tonight, we come together to honor the legacy of our beloved Secret Santa," she began, her words echoing softly in the stillness. "For years, this person, whose identity we may never know, has given us all the greatest gift of all—the gift of community. It is through the kindness of one anonymous soul that we learned what it truly means to be a part of something bigger than ourselves. And tonight, as we look to the future, we remember that spirit of giving, that spirit of love and togetherness."

There was a soft murmur of agreement from the crowd, the warmth of the sentiment settling over the gathered townsfolk. Abigail's eyes scanned the crowd, lingering on the faces of those who had known the Secret Santa most intimately—the town's elderly, the ones who had witnessed the first gift exchange decades ago, the ones who could still remember the days when the tradition had started.

"As we open this final gift tonight, we celebrate not just the person who gave it, but the spirit of giving that will continue to live on in all of us," Abigail continued. "Let us remember that the true meaning of Christmas is not in what we receive, but in what we give."

The crowd nodded in agreement, their faces a mixture of grief and hope. They all knew that once this last gift was opened, they would be saying goodbye to a tradition that had shaped their town for generations. But they were also ready to embrace something new, something inspired by the kindness and generosity that the Secret Santa had always embodied.

Abigail stepped forward to the table, where the gift waited. She took a deep breath, her fingers brushing over the smooth surface of the box. She was about to untie the ribbon when a voice called out from the back of the crowd.

"Wait!"

Everyone turned to see Martha, the town's librarian, making her way to the front. She was older now, her hair graying at the temples, but there was a fire in her eyes that hadn't dimmed with age.

"I think we all deserve to know something," she said, her voice loud enough for everyone to hear. "Before we open this gift, there's something you should know—something you won't believe, but it's true."

A murmur rippled through the crowd, and Abigail's heart skipped a beat. She knew that Martha had always been one of the town's more outspoken residents, but this was something else entirely.

"What is it, Martha?" Abigail asked, her tone steady but her mind racing.

Martha's eyes flickered nervously to the box before meeting Abigail's gaze. She took a breath, then spoke in a low, urgent voice.

"The Secret Santa... was never just one person."

There was a stunned silence. No one moved, no one spoke. The revelation hung in the air, thick and heavy.

"What do you mean?" a voice from the crowd asked.

Martha took another step forward, her voice gaining strength with each word.

"I mean, the Secret Santa was a group. A group of us."

The crowd shifted, whispers spreading like wildfire. Abigail felt her heart race as she processed what Martha was saying. She had always believed the Secret Santa to be one mysterious individual, someone who had quietly shared gifts year after year, never asking for recognition. But now, Martha was telling them something entirely different.

"There were four of us," Martha continued, her voice trembling slightly with the weight of the confession. "I was one of them. And the others..." She paused, swallowing hard before speaking again. "We've all been keeping the secret for years. It was never just one person. It was a community effort—people who believed in spreading kindness, in keeping the spirit of

Christmas alive. We would take turns, every year, placing the gifts anonymously, ensuring no one would ever know the truth."

Abigail's mind spun. The Secret Santa, the figure who had been so beloved by the town, had been a collective effort. She felt the sting of betrayal, but also something else—relief. The town hadn't lost their cherished holiday tradition. It had merely evolved, hidden behind layers of secrecy.

Martha stepped closer to the table, placing her hand on the gift.

"We all agreed that the last gift would be the one to reveal the truth. The last gift would show the town that the spirit of giving wasn't just the work of one person. It was all of us."

A ripple of emotion swept through the crowd. There were tears, and then a quiet, unified applause. They had always known the Secret Santa represented something bigger than just gifts. It was about the community, about the shared joy and love that they all contributed to.

Abigail looked down at the box, her fingers finally pulling at the ribbon. The wrapping paper fell away to reveal an old, tarnished brass key. It was simple, unassuming, but it held a weight of significance that no one had expected.

"This key," Martha said softly, "is a key to the old town hall—where the first Secret Santa gifts were given. It's a reminder that what we've shared here, in this town, is a legacy of kindness. And now, it's up to all of you to carry that forward."

As the townsfolk gathered around, the stars above twinkling brightly in the frosty sky, Abigail knew that the spirit of the Secret Santa would never truly fade. It wasn't about who gave the gifts or how they were given. It was about the heart of the community, the bond that tied them all together. And on this starry Christmas Eve, as the last gift was revealed, the true meaning of the holidays was clearer than ever before.

But then, just as the crowd began to relax and murmur among themselves, a young voice cut through the air, trembling with excitement.

"There's something else, Martha."

Abigail turned to see the voice's source—a young boy, no older than fifteen, standing in the back. He was clutching something tightly in his hand, his eyes wide with disbelief.

Martha looked over at the boy, her brow furrowing.

"What is it, Tommy?" she asked, her voice laced with confusion.

The boy took a deep breath, then slowly opened his hand. In it was a small, carefully folded note.

"This was hidden inside the key," he said.

Martha's face went pale. She reached out to take the note, her hands shaking. As she unfolded it, the message inside became clear: *The key is yours, Abigail. You were the last one who needed to know. You were the Secret Santa all along.*

The town fell silent once again. All eyes turned to Abigail, the weight of the revelation sinking in.

She had been the Secret Santa?

Her heart pounded in her chest as she looked out at the crowd, realizing that the truth had been staring her in the face all along. She had been the one to keep the tradition alive, to organize the gifts. But she had done so without ever fully realizing that she had been part of something far larger—something that had touched every person in Winter Hollow.

And now, on this starry Christmas Eve, Abigail understood. The gift wasn't just a key. It was a reminder that the community had always been the true heart of the Secret Santa, and it was their bond—stronger than any mystery—that would keep the holiday spirit alive for generations to come.